Stranger on Lesbos

VALERIE TAYLOR

AFTERWORD BY MARCIA M. GALLO

THE FEMINIST PRESS
AT THE CITY UNIVERSITY OF NEW YORK
NEW YORK CITY

Published by the Feminist Press
at the City University of New York
The Graduate Center
365 Fifth Avenue, Suite 5406
New York, NY 10016

feministpress.org

First Feminist Press edition

Text copyright © 1960 by Valerie Taylor
Afterword copyright © 2012 by Marcia M. Gallo
Originally published by Gold Medal Books in 1960

Cover and text design by Drew Stevens

Library of Congress Cataloging-in-Publication Data

Taylor, Valerie, 1913-1997.
 Stranger on Lesbos / Valerie Taylor.
   p. cm.
 ISBN 978-1-55861-799-5
 I. Title.
 PS3570.A957S87 2012
 813'.54--dc23
                    2012004437

1 STANDING IN THE DOORWAY OF THE ENGLISH CLASS-
room, Frances had a crazy feeling that the last twenty years
had dissolved and she was fifteen again, hesitating on the
threshold of the County High under the critical eyes of the town
students. She glanced down, half expecting to see cotton stockings and the cheap thick-soled oxfords from the company store,
and was reassured by the sight of her polished loafers.

She stepped into the room, already half-filled with students
and buzzing with voices. Kids are all alike, she thought, dropping into the first empty chair and arranging her purse and books
on the flaring arm. Even in a great university whose methods
were studied by educators from all over the world, somebody
had scratched initials into the wood.

The feeling of unreality swept over her again. The years of
her marriage were a dream, compressed into the time between
the mine hooter's shriek and the sizzling of fatback in the skil-
let. In a minute she would wake, facing the newspaper-covered
wall, get up and wash in a tin basin, then sit down to biscuits
and gravy.

She looked around nervously, trying to orient herself, beginning to panic. This time her gaze fell on her well-tended hands.
The past was over and gone, thank God.

She tried to concentrate on the other students. For the most
part they were young, with a thin sprinkling of middle-aged

men and women. Like me, Frances thought, and rejected the idea. No! I'm still young. I haven't really started to live yet.

The violence of her reaction frightened her. She took off the glasses she had lately begun to wear for reading, and blinked.

Her look slid over the rows of youngsters in sweaters and came to rest on a dark-haired woman in the tier of seats below her. The woman caught her eye and smiled slightly, then opened a paper-covered book and started to read. Frances studied her, ready to look away if she turned around again. She was in the late twenties, with hair more black than brown, cut short and casual. She was sturdily built, and wore her tailored white shirt as though clothes didn't interest her. The sleeves were rolled up over tanned arms. Frances thought she looked alert and intelligent, perhaps a trifle sulky, but definitely more interesting than any of the kids.

A thin graying man came in, dropped an armful of books on the lectern, and looked around the room. "My name is Kemper," he said. "In this course we are going to explore some trends in literature in the late-nineteenth and early-twentieth century, beginning with the works of D. H. Lawrence." He smiled. "Why Lawrence? Not because some of you may have heard that *Lady Chatterly's Lover* is a shocking book. But because his books, which seem so overrated and perhaps sentimental to today's critics, were the first to state in plain language the effect of human behavior of certain physical and psychic phenomena not generally conceded to exist at the time when he began to publish. Those were the good old days before Freud—or at least before the Freudians."

Some of the students laughed.

"My assistant will pass out the mimeographed reading lists at the end of the hour, but first if you will note these titles—"

Notebooks flipped open. The buzz of voices dwindled to a light hum. There was a scratching of pens.

Frances sat looking around the room, trying to adjust to this atmosphere from which she had been absent for so long.

She had been lukewarm when Bill had suggested that she register for classes at the university. "You always used to say

4

you were going back some day to get your degree. Why don't you start now?"

"Haven't thought about it in years." She had reached up to disconnect the electric toaster, begun to stack the breakfast dishes.

"I get the feeling you've been bored ever since we moved to Chicago. Women don't have enough to do around the house anymore. All these gimmicks." He looked around the sunny kitchen, frowning. "Now that Bob's in high school—"

Oh God, Frances thought, if it were only that simple. She focused on the opposite wall: refrigerator and freezer, built-in washer and dryer, all Bill's purchases, and all bought on installments. Her eyes smarted. If things were the way they used to be with us. If we ever had any time together. If we could sit down and talk things over the way we used to.

"We're doing all right," Bill said. "That last raise is going to put us in a higher tax bracket, I'm afraid." He grinned. "You can get yourself some culture if you want to."

"All right."

"Good girl." He glanced at the wall clock, snatched his attaché case from the work counter, and gave her a perfunctory kiss. "Don't forget, I may be late tonight. Big deal, buyer from Pittsburgh. Don't wait up."

He would have enough to drink before he got home—not enough to make him sodden, but too much for balance. And she would lie awake hour after hour, hearing the chimes from the Catholic church down the street and wondering miserably if, this time, entertaining an important customer would mean women. There was a class of buyer to whom a Chicago trip was an excuse for raw, commercial sex. Others were satisfied with a steak dinner, a few dirty stories, too many drinks. She'd never had any real reason to believe that Bill was unfaithful to her, but she had heard enough innuendo at parties and enough complaining from the morning coffee drinkers in the neighborhood to know what sometimes went on the expense account under "entertainment." It was a thought she couldn't push out of her mind at one in the morning.

She would lie there, dozing and waking by turns, until the late night air grew cool and pale. And finally the car would turn into the drive, headlights sweeping across the bedroom wall as they always did, and Bill's key would fumble at the front door. She would lie taut, pretending to be asleep while he undressed in the dark and crawled into bed beside her. Whether he touched her tentatively or fell at once into a heavy alcoholic sleep would depend on how much he'd had to drink and whether the customer was about ready to sign on the dotted line.

Lately he had been staying on his own side of the bed. Sometimes it seemed to her that the whole business of her marriage lay in one word: diminishing. Bill cares less for me, she thought, makes love to me less often, puts less meaning into it, and gives me less pleasure when he does. It's a gradual lessening. And with the slacking off of love (explainable on the ground of Bill's increasing preoccupation with business and his fatigue, but who can be comforted by explanation?) we're losing everything else: books, music, the practical details of learning to live together and be parents—even the nagging worry over money. Maybe it's a good thing to be broke, she thought wryly, keeps you from fretting over more important things.

She sat looking at the blank face of the back door, dimly hearing the car back out of the garage. I'll do it, she thought suddenly. I'll go over to the university this morning and get a catalogue, and maybe talk to the registrar or somebody. Why not?

She felt light and buoyant as she ran upstairs to wake Bob, their fifteen-year old son. As soon as he gets off to school, she planned, I'll shower and take the I.C. to the Midway. Bill had talked about buying a cheap secondhand car for her use and she had discouraged him, feeling that every spare dollar had to go into Bob's college account. Now she half regretted it. If I had a secondhand car, she thought, I could get to my classes without any trouble.

It felt good, having something to plan for. She caught herself humming as she zipped her skirt.

The grounds of the University of Chicago had never seemed

like a campus to her, as she glimpsed it from the windows of a bus or a train. A college ought to be a green tree-shaded expanse shut away from towns, with ivy-covered buildings and a cloistered atmosphere. Here, a series of quadrangles were flanked by the Illinois Central tracks on the east, hemmed in by grimy apartment buildings, surrounded by moldering slums of a great industrial city. But there was the same feeling of youth and optimism that had overlaid, like sunshine, the small denominational college of her youth.

She wondered which building housed the library, the old hunger for books stirring within her like a physical appetite. I belong here, she thought.

So here she was, tuition paid, a student again. It wasn't what she wanted out of life. It wasn't enough. But it was a beginning.

The instructor's voice dwindled away. She looked up from her empty notebook. The people around her were stirring, turning to speak to friends. Frances looked at her watch, a birthday gift from Bill. The hour was over. It was hard to believe, but she had wasted fifty minutes of classroom time daydreaming about a past she wanted to forget, and a future full of problems without evident solutions.

She might as well, she thought, have gone to the movies.

I'd have been half crazy with excitement in the old days, she reproached herself, remembering her arrival at Wallace with her belongings in a borrowed suitcase (and a black eye—yes, but that was a symbol of the evil and ugliness she was leaving behind, and so it had a part in her new freedom, too). In her shabby purse was a neatly typed envelope with the return address of the college in the corner, in it the letter confirming her scholarship. She carried the same purse three years later, when she stood before a strange minister with Bill Ollenfield and promised to love, honor, and obey.

Now she got to her feet, gathering up her belongings. I was young then, she thought sadly, and in love. Love. At twenty, it's thrills in the moonlight. At thirty-five it's remembering to send his shirts to the laundry.

Going out into the talk-echoing corridor, she fell into step

7

with the dark-haired young woman she had noticed earlier. They looked at each other intently for a moment, and Frances felt the color rise in her cheeks. She smiled uncertainly. The other girl gave her a questioning look, then smiled back and walked swiftly away. Frances stood watching her until she was lost in the crowd, wondering who she was and why she was in school.

2 HER ONLY WORRY WHEN THEY HAD MOVED TO CHI-cago a year earlier, had been about Bob. Not about Bill, who was wrapped up in his job. His work for the welfare board had become more and more perfunctory over the preceding four or five years: the people listed on his neat index cards were only case histories to him, and he was tired of trying to stretch a social worker's salary to cover the increasing cost of living. He was a young man still, but the early zest, the bounce, had gone out of him.

True, he had been first indifferent and then undecided when his Uncle Walter had offered him a job as sales manager for Plastic Playthings, at approximately twice what he had been earning; but he had decided for it, as he surely would not have done five years earlier. And she had to admit, dubious as she was at first, that he was making good. He got along with the gray-flannel-suit people, the martini-with-lunch crowd, and his two salary increases had little to do with his being the owner's nephew. He was *in*.

As for her—well, you can wash dishes anywhere.

The child psychology books all emphasized the importance of security for a child, especially during adolescence. She laughed, pulling a soft sweater over her head. Bob, entering high school as a sophomore, had fit into the new life with no bother at all. Now he looked and acted just like his classmates at South Shore High and was hardly ever at home.

Adolescence, she thought a little bitterly, stooping to choose a pair of shoes from the closet floor. I don't have to worry about him. He doesn't need me anymore than his father does. Anybody who could cook would do just as well. Good old mom, a standard piece of household equipment.

The thought sprang into her mind, unwelcome: nobody needs me. Bill's at the office or out with a customer most of the time, mixing business with pleasure. He never opens a book anymore, doesn't care about the theater, doesn't even talk about getting a hi-fi, now that we could afford one. And how long has it been since we really talked together? You can't count all those arguments about the grocery bills.

She picked up her handbag, decided against a jacket, and ran slightly down the stairs. Her work was done. The house was in order. It was an easy house to care for, smaller than the one Bill had wanted—he'd been all for buying a place in the suburbs, where they could have a garden and an outdoor grill, and entertain his business contacts. That meant living a little beyond their means and being always worried about the unpaid bills, like most of the couples she had met since they moved. She was glad she'd stood firm. The bank account for Bob's education was more important than anything else.

Bill had gone ahead and bought the new car, the wide-screen TV, and the three new suits—after all, a sales manager can't wear slacks and an old tweed jacket. But she had won on the question of the house, which stood in a decent but not smart neighborhood, and had only two bedrooms.

We don't even have enough in common to quarrel, she thought. What Bill really needs is somebody like Betty Flanagan, who really likes backyard barbecues and doesn't mind when someone tells traveling salesman stories. Who tells them herself, for that matter, and kisses other people's husbands at parties.

It would be nice to have someone to talk to.

She stepped up into the bus and dropped her quarter into the fare box.

This time the campus seemed to welcome her, as if she had a right to be there. She walked along briskly, pleased and a little excited at the prospect of the hour ahead, and wondering if she would recognize any of her classmates. If she would ever come to know any of them as friends.

The dark-haired girl she had noticed the first day was already there, reading. She welcomed Frances with a smile and motioned to an empty chair beside her own. Frances sat down and said, "Hi. How are you getting along with the reading list?"

"It's mostly review," the other said. She closed the book, keeping a finger in her place. Frances noticed that it wasn't a library copy, but a paperback volume that looked as though it had been read not once but many times. "He's good though—Kemper, not Lawrence. Have you had him before?"

Frances felt ashamed to admit that this was her first time in a classroom in fifteen years, that she was just a housewife smothered by walls and trying to find—what?—she didn't know. She said hesitantly, "No, we're new here. We've been living in Pennsylvania, my husband and son and I." She blushed. It sounded terribly stuffy.

"I'm working on my M. A. I may not live to make it, but it's fun trying." Frances liked the girl's quick self-deriding smile. "I'm Mary Baker, by the way. I have a crazy job—television promotion."

"That sounds exciting."

"It's a living."

"Anything is better than washing dishes," Frances said. "Miss Baker—or is it Mrs. Baker?"

"Miss. My friends call me Bake."

"I'm Frances Ollenfield." And what did names matter, Frankie Kirby or Mrs. William Ollenfield, when you met someone you really liked? "Look," she said, "why does the instructor start with Lawrence?"

"He said why. Because Lawrence was the first to express what other people knew but were afraid to give words to," Mary Baker said. "Sex, of course, but other things too. He knew how people really feel about things, not how they think they ought to feel. He helped smash the old taboos. That's why he's great, even if he did write badly sometimes."

"He's dated."

"Yes." Bake's face hardened. "Not as much as you think, though. We've got a long way to go."

Frances looked down at her hands. "Did you get to the place where Mrs. Morel sits in the garden, wondering where her life has gone to—feeling as though her whole life had been lived by somebody else?"

"I remember it: Do you feel like that?"

The answer came so simply that she had no time to be embarrassed. "Sometimes."

"It's a great pity," Bake said softly. "Life is so short, it's too bad not to get the most out of every single second."

Easier said than done, Frances thought.

Through the class hour she kept stealing looks at the girl beside her. A stranger. But not a stranger somehow; like someone known before, and to be better known. She liked Bake's clear, firm profile under the short hair, her good nose and solid chin, the way her neck rose out of the white collar. She liked the way Bake sat with her shoulders back and her feet firmly planted. By contrast, Frances felt colorless and insipid.

It seemed natural to have Bake suggest that they go out for a drink when the class hour was over. This was like high school—girls wandering off to the snack shop or soda fountain after hours. (But not skinny, shabby, little Frankie Kirby from the mines, ever.) They went to a little place just off campus, and Bake ordered martinis.

"But I don't drink."

"You'll have to learn. You need to loosen up."

The drink was cold and faintly bitter. It made Frances feel alert and relaxed at the same time. She listened while Bake talked about books, about Lawrence. "Read *The Rainbow*. It's not on Kemper's list, but it's one of the best." She mentioned an argument she had with a man who had known Lawrence in New Mexico, a newspaperman whose syndicated columns Frances read every week. "You meet all kinds of people on a job like mine. Some of the famous ones are slobs. But some are fascinating."

"It sounds wonderful."

"It's all right."

Four girls came in together and sat down at the next table. One gave Bake a curious look, raised a hand in greeting, then turned away. Bake's mouth hardened. "I've got to be going. Can I drop you somewhere?"

"Oh no, the bus is handy."

"Come on, I'll drive you home."

She drove fast and well. Frances, who usually sat clutching the edge of the seat if Bill went over fifty, realized that they were well over the speed limit, but she felt no anxiety. They took the short drive in companionable silence. When they drew up in front of her house, she found herself looking at it through Bake's eyes: a stodgy middle-class dwelling for dull people.

"I hate this place," Frances said. "But what can you do—with the housing shortage."

"It doesn't matter. I'll see you Friday."

Frances felt her face grow warm. "I'll buy *you* a drink then."

"Good enough."

Bake waved, turned her car around skillfully, and sped away, her left arm hanging negligently out of the open window. Frances stood watching until she turned the corner. Then she went inside, feeling more exhilarated than one drink could account for, and knelt down in front of the bookcase to look for *The Rainbow.*

3 I THOUGHT YOU WEREN'T COMING."

"I had lunch with a client. God, I thought I'd never break away." Bake undid the top button of her jacket and puffed a deep breath indicating how she had hurried. "I wanted to see you even if I didn't make it to class. Did I miss anything?"

"Pop quiz." Frances caught the waiter's eye. He gave her a token smile and came over. "You can easily make it up."

"Sometimes I wonder if it's worth the trouble. I've been doing this for years and years, all to get two little letters after my name."

"No classes Friday."

"Of course not, Thanksgiving weekend."

"I'll miss seeing you."

"I suppose you'll have a big family dinner, with turkey and so on?"

"I'm afraid so."

Frances remembered, with a nostalgic pang, the first Thanksgiving after she and Bill were married. There wasn't any money for turkey; they were saving every nickel to pay for the baby. Bill came home from work with a sparrow feather, which he stuck solemnly on top of the meatloaf. She sighed.

"What's the matter?"

"Nothing really. I was just thinking how conventional people get as they grow older."

"Age has nothing to do with it. Most people are born conventional."

"I'll miss going to the university on Friday," Frances said.

The waiter set their drinks down. She took hers absentmindedly. "Bill will be out of town all day and Bob's never home anymore. If it isn't ham radio it's basketball."

"It's going to be a good day to get out into the country, if the weather holds." Bake glanced out into the street where a few late leaves rattled dryly along the sidewalk. The sky was blue, the sun bright. "Of course we could have a blizzard, but this is certainly unusual weather for November." She studied Frances above the rim of her glass. "Why don't we both take the day off and go for a drive. We could bring sandwiches."

Frances would have been willing to spend the day on a rock pile with a pickax if Bake had suggested it. Anything was better than wandering around an empty house, dusting furniture that was already clean and wondering what Bill was doing and when he would get home.

"That sounds like fun."

"Good. The woods out around Elgin ought to be gorgeous by now. I'll call you Thursday night and we can settle the details."

They separated, Bake to keep an appointment with a client, Frances to sit at the table a while longer, in a haze of well-being that came partly from gin and partly from being with Bake. A whole day together, away from other people and their demands—a day without assignments or obligations. It was more than she could accept. She was afraid to believe in it.

She thought back over the scattered hours she and Bake had spent together in the last few weeks. Brief as the encounters were, impersonal as their talks had been, they gave depth and color to the day. When Bake missed a class, as happened now and then, Frances felt flat and let down.

Now, turning the empty glass in her fingers, she tried prudently to brace herself against disappointment. She'll change her mind, she thought. Or it will snow or something. Don't count on going.

But she was smiling as she paid the cashier and went out into the crisp autumnal sunshine, warning herself: she won't call. Frances knew better.

Bake called at eleven the next night, just three hours after the Flanagans "dropped in for a minute" and while they were having one last drink, which was likely to stretch into three or four. Frances said, "Excuse me," and lifted the phone from its cradle, wishing desperately that she had succumbed to the telephone company's urging and had an extension installed in the kitchen. Betty Flanagan let her story trail off, listening.

"Hello?"

"This is Bake. Didn't get you out of bed or anything, did I?"

"No. Just sitting here talking to some people."

"Oh, then you're not free to talk."

"No."

"Look, suppose I pick you up around nine? I'll take care of the lunch. Wear something durable. We'll look for bittersweet." A burst of music drowned her out. Frances waited. Bake's voice returned, sounding far away and full of laughter. "I'm in Hal Butler's apartment with ten thousand crazy people, mostly looped. Look, baby, I'll see you in the morning. Right?"

"Right," Frances hung up. "That was a girl in my class at the university," she said, coming back to sit beside Betty but looking at Bill. "I'm going for a drive in the country with some people I know tomorrow."

"Do you good," Jack Flanagan said generously. "Hey, Bill, anything left in the pitcher?"

"Might be a small dividend."

"How about you, Frances?"

"Frances doesn't drink," Bill said. "She's a culture vulture—Shakespeare and the opera."

"No vices," Betty Flanagan said. She crossed her knees so that her sheath skirt slipped a little higher. Bill poured another drink and leaned across the sofa to hand it to her, flicking a look down her scoop neckline.

Jack Flanagan said, "Get with it, woman. Bill and I have to get up early and go to Milwaukee tomorrow."

Betty winked at Frances. "We know what they're going to do in Milwaukee, don't we?"

"It's a great town," Bill said. "All that beer, all those big busty blondes."

"Maybe I'll go on your picnic, Fran. Any attractive men?"

"Just girls. Anyway, there's no room."

"Aah, nuts."

Frances was silent. Why did I lie, she asked herself, honestly puzzled. I don't want Betty trailing along, of course. But there's no reason I can't go somewhere with just one girl. No reason at all to feel so—well, illicit. As if I had a secret date with a man.

She saw the Flanagans to the door, her silence unnoticed in the flurry of goodnights, and came back shivering into the warm house.

"Do you really have to go to Milwaukee tomorrow, Bill?"

He looked surprised. "Sure, this is a big account. This guy buys all the toys for one of the biggest department stores in town. No telling what time we'll get back."

She stood on tiptoe to put her arms around his neck.

"Remember the first Thanksgiving we had together?"

"I remember we were damn hard up."

But not the laughter, or the way we fell into bed when the

dishes were done, in the middle of the afternoon, because we couldn't wait. That was the first time I ever really—she blinked.

"Better hit the sack, honey," Bill said. "I'll be upstairs pretty soon."

He honestly didn't remember.

Upstairs, she undressed mechanically and put on her pajamas. Then, in a resurgence of hope, she stripped them off and stuffed them into the hamper. From a bottom drawer she took a sheer black nylon nightgown she had never worn, a present from Bill after a recent sales convention. (Guilty conscience? She pushed the thought out of her mind.) A dab of perfume under her arms and bosom and behind her knees, a quick brushing out of her hair, and she was ready. She lay tense, waiting.

The clock struck one.

From the foot of the stairs came the rustling of paper and the light scratch of a pen. She blinked furiously. He was down there mapping out his Milwaukee campaign, going over the plans he and Jack Flanagan had made this afternoon, while she lay here ready and waiting. She jumped out of bed.

From the head of the stairs she could see him, surrounded by catalogues and price lists. "Bill, please come to bed."

He looked up absently. "In a minute, hon, I'm busy."

If I were like Betty Flanagan, she thought, I'd go out and get myself another man. As all wives do at times, she tried to imagine herself in a lover's embrace, but the picture refused to take form and she gave it up.

She sat on the edge of the bed, waiting.

Darling, she thought—mentally addressing a younger and more responsive Bill—I don't want to get ahead in the world. Honestly, I don't. I know you're doing this for Bobby and me, but all we really need is to be the way we used to be. To share things, and to go for walks together, and listen to records. To be together.

The mature Bill, downstairs, rumpled a sheet of paper and threw it into the wastebasket. It landed with a soft plop.

Men, Frances thought resentfully, pulling the pillow up

around her ears to shut out the rustling of papers from down-stairs. Never trust a man. They always let you down when you need them most.

Like pain flowing back into an old scar, the memory of Freddie Fischer stirred in her. Freddie, the three-letter man and senior-class hero, the boy no girl ever said no to; Freddie, who sat in the back row of the senior English class not because he was shy, like her, but because he preferred not to catch the teacher's eye. Let other, less gifted men worry about Chaucer and the Lake poets. He had glory and glamour, and he had women.

He could have had her, anytime. Homely little Frankie Kirby, with her stringy hair and faded cotton dresses—and her straight-A record. He had taken her home from school half a dozen times in his red convertible, letting her out at the corner so her father wouldn't know. Had kissed her casually, and let her write his term papers and book reports. Had invited her to the homecoming dance after his eligibility for the football team was finally secure, and had left her waiting for him to appear, corsage in hand. She still hoped that he had meant to go through with it—that it had been a fleeting generosity and not a crude joke.

Because that night had cost her much. She had stolen the money for a formal, a permanent wave, high-heeled slippers and fancy earrings from her father's overall pocket while he slept, without a qualm except for the chance of his waking and catching her. Had been ready and eager to park with Freddie or go to a motel with him, or, in short, do anything he wanted her to.

Maybe, she had thought—putting on the net dress with the sequined ruffles, teetering unsteadily on the tall heels—maybe he'll even ask me to marry him. For it was 1941 and high school boys were marrying their classmates, marrying girls met in bars and dime stores, marrying anyone in their frenzy to experience love and leave children behind before they went off to be killed.

She didn't know until the next day that he had patched up

a fight with his real girl after the game, three hours before she changed into the net dress; that he was dancing with Patty Kelly, holding her tighter than the chaperones approved of and whispering into her ear, while she sat on the porch, until the morning sun reddened the sky and she went inside and went to bed, but not to sleep. I'll never sleep again, she thought in her proud and hurt young ignorance. The sequins on her dress winked at her from the rough pine floor.

Who cares how a miner's kid feels, a girl from Frisbie, that tangle of wooden cottages and slag heaps on the edge of town?

The grown-up Frances turned restlessly between wrinkled sheets, dry-mouthed and tense, even now, under the memory of that rebuff.

But Bill isn't like that. Bill's good and kind, and he loves me.

Past tense. Used to be kind. Used to love me.

(The small hotel room, small-town hotel at its worst, she knew now, had been blessed by his gentleness and patience. Even though he could not have known, that night of their hasty and ill-considered marriage, why she was afraid. She had started to tell him, "The night my mother died—" and had faltered to a stop, with his eyes questioningly on her face.)

Mixed with remembered shame, now, was the growing, insistent pressure of desire, a dim feeling, of need at first, sharpening to a definitive, insistent urge. She sat up in bed, hating herself for needing him, hating him for humiliating her this way.

"Bill," she called.

"What's the matter?" His voice was loud and cheerful—a salesman's voice, she thought. She said hesitantly, "I can't sleep."

"Take a phenobarb. Some in the medicine chest."

Her eyes widened. She sat irresolute, waiting. Bill's chair scraped across the floor. "Don't wait up for me. I'll be a little while."

"Oh, to hell with it," Frances said aloud. She pulled the covers up under her chin and lay silent for a long time, staring at nothing.

4 BAKE TURNED THE HANDLE THAT OPENED THE CAR door. "You look a little shadowy. Company stay late?"

"Late enough. They were just some people Bill knows." Frances took a deep breath, feeling better. "One of the salesmen and his wife."

"What's your son doing?"

"Spending the day with a friend."

Bake stripped off her leather-palmed gloves and wadded them down behind the seat. "Damn it, I liked to get my hands into things." She gave Frances a look at once sharp and concerned. "Relax, baby. We're going to get out of traffic and get a little fresh air."

The highway was a long white ribbon unrolling before them, with a few cars scuttling like insects. "Not much traffic," Bake said. She lit a cigarette. "Sunday will be terrible, but everybody's hung over today."

They rode as they always did, without talking.

A few miles south of Elgin, Bake turned off the highway. They picked their way over a gravel road edged with drying brown weeds. Crows flew up, shrieking, at the car's approach. A woman hanging clothes on a backyard line looked after them curiously. Bake took the car to the end of the road, which dwindled out in a clump of trees. Beyond a sagging barbed wire fence was a thick stand of shagbark hickories, reaching as far as Frances could see in three directions. She turned an inquiring look upon Bake.

"It's like this for miles, all along the riverbank. Virgin timber, the way it was when the Indians lived here."

"It's quiet, isn't it?"

They were still. Far away a dog barked. Single leaves fell slowly, turning in the breeze.

"Hungry?" Bake asked.

"Not so very."

"I've got sandwiches and a thermos of coffee and some Scotch. Hal gave me the Scotch—it ought to be good." She stretched luxuriously. "God, this is beautiful. I thought we might cook dinner at my place, if you want to. If we feel like going back and cooking, we will. If we don't, we can eat along the way. There's no hurry."

"I'd like to see your apartment."

"No hurry," Bake said again. "Let's see what it's like in the wilderness."

Frances climbed through the barbed wire fence, wishing she had worn slacks. Bake stood beside her, neatly trousered and sweatered, the wind ruffling her short dark hair. They looked at each other. Then a red squirrel ran up a tree, jabbering and scolding and Bake laughed.

"Come on. I bet there's bittersweet in some of these old fence corners, and you hardly ever find it growing wild anymore."

The brown leaves crackled under their shoes.

It was almost evening when they climbed through the fence again, holding the rusted strands apart for each other. Frances was tired, but exhilarated. She laid her armful of scarlet sumac, bittersweet, and late maple leaves on the back seat while Bake turned the hickory nuts out of her jacket pockets. They sat down in the car, side by side, breathless and smiling. Frances was conscious for the first time that her shoes were wet and muddy, her hands stained with hickory hulls and barbed wire rust. She laughed.

Bake sat with her hands on the steering wheel, not making any move to start the car. "Do you realize that we haven't eaten all day? I'm starving."

"I could use coffee."

"Here, let me." Bake got the top off the thermos, slopping coffee over the edge of the plastic cup. "Put a little whiskey in it. It'll warm you up."

"I'm not cold."

"Let's go up to my place and cook a real meal. Let's not take the edges off our appetites with sandwiches."

Frances sipped the coffee and scotch, feeling dreamily agreeable to anything Bake might suggest.

"Lovely," she murmured.

"Hey, you're falling asleep."

"I am not."

"Lean your head against my shoulder if you want to. We'll be home in an hour."

"You won't get sleepy?"

"No," Bake said smiling, "I won't get sleepy."

Frances could feel the car start. Her knees braced automatically against the jar as they lurched back on to the gravel road. Then she laid her head against Bake's soft wool sweater, feeling the good solidity of bone and the warmth of living flesh beneath. The western sky was darkly pink against a bank of curly gray cloud. It was too much for one time. She sank down into a half-sleep, unwilling to relinquish consciousness but unable to stay fully awake.

"Your hair smells nice," Bake said. She shifted to lay an arm across Frances's shoulders, whether for support or reassurance was not clear. She's driving with her left hand, Frances thought foggily, but then she felt no alarm. She had utter confidence in Bake's ability to do anything she set out to do.

Then without any apparent passage of time they were stopping in front of a brick apartment building. Frances struggled upright and sat looking owlishly at the street lights, the passing cars, and the close-set buildings.

"Here we are," Bake said. "Pull yourself together and see if you can get out."

Electric light beat down on the lobby floor, set with black-and-white tile squares meant to look like marble. Bake unlocked the mailbox under her name card, found nothing, and unlocked the inner door. They climbed a flight of stairs, their wet shoes squishing on the thin carpeting, and walked down a long hall past a double row of closed doors.

"It's not very chic," Bake said, "but it's in easy commuting distance of most of my clients—and anyways I'd rather spend money on books." It was not an apology. She laid her double armful of leaves and berries on the hall floor and fished in a pocket for her door key.

"Oh, you carried my stuff up too."

"That's all right."

"What a nice room!" Frances said as they entered.

The living room looked larger than it was because it was sparsely furnished and almost bare of decoration. A chair of woven leather strips and one of steel mesh flanked a nondescript studio couch with a Mexican blanket laid across it. The walls were lined with brick-and-plank bookshelves.

"You can look at the books as soon as you get your wet shoes off," Bake said, smiling.

A Navajo rug punctuated the flat black of the floor, and the windows were covered with inside blinds painted dark green. Best of all, there was a working fireplace, the brick hearth dusted lightly with ashes. Bake crumpled a sheet of newspaper, knelt to arrange it with three sticks, and lit one of the kitchen matches she carried in her shirt pocket. A tiny blaze leapt up, primitive in its beauty.

"What is it about fire?"

"It's a symbol," Bake said. "Home and safety—and other things too." She snapped on a light in the adjoining bedroom, plunged into the closet, and came back carrying a pair of soft slippers with elastic bands across the instep. "You're taller than I am, but I have bigger feet. Maybe you can keep these on."

"They're so soft."

"They're an acrobat's practice shoes."

She wondered how Bake happened to have them, but she didn't want to ask.

"Sit down in front of the fire. I'll fix us a drink before I start the steaks."

Frances was looking dreamily into the flames when Bake came back with two full glasses. "Here, now let's put a real chunk of wood on the fire. Are you in any hurry to go home?"

"No," Frances said. She opened her eyes wide, smiled contentedly at Bake. "I'd like to stay here forever. I don't know why I used to think drinking wine was a vice," Frances said, sliding down a little deeper into the cushions and flexing her toes in the thin slippers. "I feel wonderful."

"Maybe that's why," Bake suggested. "Life is real, life is earnest, and all that jazz. We can't have people going around here all full of euphoria." She sounded a little vague, and her eyes narrowed as they always did after a couple of drinks. She set her glass on the floor with exaggerate care.

"Just as soon be full of euphoria, if it means what I think it does." Frances got up and walked to a bookcase. The bindings of the books, all soft bright colors, blurred a little in the flickering light from the fireplace. Bake had turned off all but one lamp, a small one on the corner of the desk, "so you can't see where I burned the steak." Now Frances said, pleased, "Oh, here's *The Rainbow.* I did read it, you know."

"You didn't tell me. How did you like it?"

Frances hesitated. She could find no words for the mixture of puzzlement and revelation she had felt, as though some truth unsuspected this far was about to be revealed with the next page she turned.

"I'm not sure. I didn't understand some of it very well."

Bake looked at her intently. "What didn't you understand?"

"Oh, a lot of it." She took a restless step. "The fire's going out."

"I'll have to order more wood before you come again. Remind me, will you?"

"Good heavens, it can't be twelve o'clock."

"It probably is. I'll take you home if you really feel you have to go. Another drink first?"

"Please."

Frances wandered back to the studio couch and sat dreamily looking at nothing special, content to be there. Definitely, she thought, I've had too much to drink already. It's kind of a nice feeling, though—everything soft and fuzzy around the edges. She accepted the glass Bake brought from the kitchen. They sat side by side, drinking slowly, not talking. She felt rather than saw the warm solidity of Bake's thigh next to hers on the cushion and the even rise in her chest.

"You're the nicest person I know," she said sleepily, hearing her voice wobbly and small.

"I like you too. Very much."

"I wish you could be my roommate in college, or something."

"Do you?" Bake got up and walked slowly across the room, glass in hand, leaving emptiness where she had been. Frances looked unhappily at her back. "I didn't mean—" She fell silent, because she was not sure, herself, what she had or hadn't meant.

"Look here. When you read *The Rainbow,* did you get to the part where Ursula and Winifred go down to the water together, in the darkness, before the storm?"

"Yes, but—"

"That's the part you didn't understand, isn't it?"

Frances was miserably silent, turning her glass around and around in her hand."

"Isn't it?"

"Well, yes."

"Frances, didn't you ever hear of women loving each other?"

Frances jumped up and went to stand beside her. "Look, Bake, that's not what I was thinking about. I mean, you don't have to worry about anything like that. I'm not like that." She seized Bake's hand in both of hers, almost crying. "Honestly, I don't even know what they—look, Bake, please don't give it another thought."

Bake pulled her hand away. "People do feel that way sometimes, you know. It happens quite often."

"I know, but don't worry about it. Even if I felt that way about you, I wouldn't say anything about it. Or make any trouble for you. I mean, I'd get over it. So that's all right."

Bake stood looking away from her, pondering, like a grown-up trying to put an abstract idea into terms a child can understand. "You don't know what I'm talking about, do you?"

"Do you mean—"

"For God's sake, don't you ever finish a sentence?" Bake moved away abruptly. She walked back to the couch and sat down, stretching out her legs in mud-splashed navy slacks.

"I do get into the goddamnedest situations."

"Bake, please."

"I love you." Bake said quietly. "I think I've loved you for quite a while. Come on, I'll take you home now."

Frances's eyes widened. They looked at each other steadily.

She came and stood awkwardly beside Bake, wanting to touch her but afraid to.

"I don't want to go home. I think I love you too."

"You don't know what you're talking about."

"I know how I feel. You could show me."

"I've always sworn I wouldn't do this," Bake said in a low harsh voice. She bent her head. "Apparently there are some things you can't help. They just happen."

"Will you let me stay?"

"Yes, of course. I don't seem to have any choice."

"You won't hate me if I'm—scared or clumsy?"

"Oh, good God."

They came into each other's arms like puppets moved by a single string. In the faint light from the desk lamp, Frances saw Bake's eyes close tightly, as though to shut away every sensation but touch. "I love you," she said again, and raised her mouth to Bake's in hunger and anticipation.

5 YOU HAVE TO GO HOME NOW."

"I know." Frances raised upon one elbow, watching Bake as she moved around the bedroom. "I don't want to."

"But you have to." Bake's smile bought small creases to the corners of her eyes. "Come on, don't stop to think about it. The longer you put it off, the worse it gets."

"I wish I didn't ever have to go."

"Me too."

Her clothes lay where she had dropped them, on the floor beside her bed. She stopped to pick them up, and was at once aware of her body, as she had never been with Bill. As though she had been thinking along the same lines, Bake asked, "Will you run into trouble at home?"

"How can I have trouble? I called. It's not my fault there was nobody there."

But she wondered how she could hide the experiences of that night. She got up and looked into the dressing-table mirror, seeing her color deeper and her eyes brighter, a thin veil of boredom or resignation—the habit of years, a thing she had come to carry without being aware of it—stripped away. She looked like a girl; and she was glad, not for the sake of vanity but because she was a little older than Bake and afraid that the extra years would come between them.

She said, "I wish I were beautiful."

Bake came to look into the mirror too, as though the reflection might give back a deeper truth than warm flesh. "You are," she said seriously. "You have a beautiful sensitive mouth and winged eyebrows."

"I look like everybody else."

"You look like my Frankie."

She stepped into the shower reluctantly, feeling that the warm water must wash off Bake's touch and leave her again the sterile, neutral creature she had been before last night.

Don't think about Bill.

Bake followed her into the bathroom. "Are you going to start feeling guilty about your husband?"

Frances's eye widened. "I don't think so. He doesn't want me anyhow, he's all wrapped up in his work." Was it only two nights ago that she had lain wide-eyed until almost morning, rebuffed and hurt? "I don't care, though."

"I haven't got any other obligations, you see," Bake said. "I haven't had for quite a while now."

Frances looked at the familiar classroom Bake in a skirt and tailored blouse, drawing a bright-red mouth over soft pink lips. "Am I going to see you again? I don't mean at school."

"As soon as we can manage it. Frances—you're not mad at me, are you?"

"Because you made me do it? Oh no. I didn't mean to get scared. That was stupid," Frances said gravely. She sat holding the soaped washcloth, looking up at Bake with big eyes. "Only it was the first time."

"Don't remind me." Bake went into the bedroom and came back with a pair of shoes. She bent to put them on, her face averted. "I'm not going to ask you what I want to ask."

"You don't have to."

"And so?"

"As good as it ever was with—anybody else. I mean, it's not like in books anyhow, at least not much of the time." She paused, remembering the routine encounters of her married nights and the others, fewer, that were something special. "You do it and everything's all right, but not so wonderful. At least—well, I don't know."

"Sometimes it is," Bake said softly. "I promise you will be better next time, when you're not scared. Come on, let's have some breakfast."

"I don't want anything but coffee. I would love some coffee."

They parted at the front door without a word or a touch, Frances watching Bake's cab carry her away to an early morning appointment. When the cab was out of sight she thriftily took a bus.

Bob was in the kitchen, all wrists and ankles below his pajamas, when she let herself in. He had cooked a vast plateful of bacon and eggs and was putting bread in the electric toaster.

"Hi, Mom. Where were you?"

"Staying with a girl I know. And where were you at midnight, young man? I phoned home and nobody answered."

"Oh heck, we stayed to see the show twice. *Midnight Horrow* and *The Ghoul from Outer Space*. It was really cool." He took a long drink of milk, wiping his mouth on his pajama sleeve. "Dad went to a Saturday sales conference. I made him some joe."

"Thanks, boy scout."

She went upstairs and sat for a long time on the edge of the unmade bed. She felt only hopeful and completely alive. This is infidelity, she told herself as she stood at the bus stop with an armful of books on Monday morning; I'm being unfaithful. And then: oh, nonsense. The words were meaningless.

Maybe if I were involved with some man, she thought. But she couldn't imagine it.

In fifteen years of marriage, she had never felt the slightest interest in any other man. For that matter, love, even as she explored it with Bill, had been a letdown. Marriage, so mysteri-

27

ous and desirable to a young inexperienced girl, turned out to be a matter of routine when the novelty wore off—not the grim sordid business she had seen it in her cramped and impoverished girlhood, but not magic either.

But this—this loving someone like yourself, who knew what you wanted and how to give it to you! She felt her mouth curling into a smile, remembering the response Bake had wrung from her in spite of her fright and ineptness.

She boarded her bus and sat hugging her books, beaming at the commonplace houses and stores as they slid by. For all the pleasure of remembering, she was a little shy about facing Bake. Reliving the hours in Bake's bed, she felt that the whole thing had been a dream. Things like this don't happen. I can't believe it. She took her accustomed chair and sat looking at the floor, with trembling knees and pounding heart, until Bake came in and sat down beside her, looking just as she always did. Then the fright dissolved. She felt cool and calm.

"Hi."

"Hi."

"Everything all right with you?"

"Everything is fine with me."

"Really?"

"Sure."

Down between the chairs, Bake's hand brushed hers so lightly that the touch might have been an accident. "We might stay down for lunch, if you're free."

"That would be fine." The ruled lines of Frances's notebook came into focus; the instructor's voice, which had been an inane buzz above Bake's whispering, made sense again. Everything was all right.

6 SO THEN WHAT HAPPENED?"

"Oh, I don't know," Frances said a little vaguely. She came back to the present, looking around the living room with a slightly dazed expression. "I talk too much."

"No, its fascinating." Bake stood up, carried the coffee cups into the kitchen, and brought them back full and steaming. "I mean, you read about things like that, but I've never known anyone it really happened to."

"It's nothing to brag about," Frances said shortly.

"Poor baby. I wish I'd known you then."

"But I had books. And then when I got into high school there was Miss Putnam." Tenderness crept into her voice. Miss Putnam, angular and strict like a comic-strip schoolteacher; where was she now? "She got me a scholarship to go to college," Frances said, cradling her cup in both hands and watching the tendrils of steam curl up into the warm air of the room. "A little denominational college where she'd gone. She knew somebody on the board, I think. She paid for my books and bought me a pair of shoes and lent me a suitcase to put my clothes in."

Ma had been pleased and excited. She sat up against the pillow, color coming to her face that had been pinched with pain since the last baby was born dead. "You go, Frankie. Don't let anything stand in your way. Not anything!"

"Who'll take care of things here?"

"Never mind. It's your chance."

Remembering, she laughed harshly. "My father whipped me when I told him. He'd have killed me, I guess if Ma hadn't threatened to call the sheriff. It's the only time I ever saw her stand up to him."

Bake's mouth was soft. She laid a comforting hand on Frances's arm. "You've had a rough time."

"It's all right."

"How come you didn't finish college? Miss Whatsername run out of money, or something?"

"My mother died. It took her a long time to die. Cancer."

Put like this, it seemed incredible that any human being could agonize as she had done in those gray barren weeks after her mother's burial, crushed under the load of housework and despairing of ever getting free, cut off from the education that was her only way of escape, loaded with the knowledge that if she had stayed at home, her mother's suffering might have been lightened. Not ended—no, it was too late for that—but sometimes, as she mopped endless floors and wrung clothes out of the soapy water, it seemed to her that no sacrifice would have been too much if it could have spared her mother one hour of that eating, animal-like pain.

"Then Ma's brother came to see us," she said slowly, "and took the kids home to his farm."

She had been scrubbing the kitchen floor when Uncle Will Schroeder showed up at the back door and announced, as if it were an everyday thing to work miracles, that he was restoring her to life. Frankie had fainted against his chest, and come to with his firm calloused hand on her wrist, his honest eyes fixed on her face.

Her lips curved. "Then at college I met Bill. He was taking courses for extra credit—he was a case worker for the state welfare board."

"It sounds like a soap opera."

"I don't suppose people would listen to soap operas if they weren't real, sort of. I mean, these things happen."

"What I can't figure out," Bake said, "is how Bill ever talked you into marrying him. What happened—you get pregnant or something?"

Frances reddened. It was close enough to the truth; she needn't have worried, as it turned out, but she had worried for two solid weeks after that uncomfortable and embarrassing night in the local hotel, and Bill had gone on urging her, and—she sat upright. "Look, do we have to talk about me all the time?"

"I'm interested," Bake said. "Aren't you glad I'm interested?"

"Yes, of course. Only it's five o'clock, and I have to go home and cook dinner."

"And there may be someone there to eat it, or again, there may not." Bake's face was blank; she kept her voice flat, without expression.

Frances stood up. "I have to go just the same."

"Meet me for lunch tomorrow? Same place."

"All right."

She was surprised, whenever she thought about it, to realize how little time they actually spent together. Bake had a job. Frances had forgotten how time consuming even a freelance job can be, compared with the flexible schedule of a housewife whose child is in school.

Although Bake talked about her work slightingly, she took it seriously and devoted a great deal of time and effort to it. In her spare time she attended a handicraft class and two university courses. She also gave an evening every week to the children's wing of a big hospital, working with post-polio patients. Her hands were strong and sure, she was unsentimental and brisk, and Frances was surprised to find that she seemed rather ashamed of this service.

"Always thought I'd like to be a physiotherapist," Bake said at lunch one day.

"You make me feel so useless. I don't have enough to do."

"I always thought these overworked housewives were kidding themselves," Bake said with a smile. She laid her purse and gloves on the table and leaned back looking around the crowded dining room. "That's Robert Flynn, the public relations man for Midwestern Electric Manufacturing. The blonde with him is a secretary in a Loop law firm. I met her at a publisher's open house; one of her bosses had a book published a few years ago. He was interviewed on *Book News and Views*."

"You know everybody, don't you?"

"Well, people are just people anyplace you go. I sort of like this crazy mixed-up town, though."

Francs shook her head. She felt that people who had their names in the paper were different, more important, more glamorous. Bake laughed. "You're as intelligent as any of them, more than most. I'll introduce you to some of the headliners if you want me to. You'll see."

She wanted to reach across the table and touch the hand that held Bake's glass, make some mute sign of love.

As the weeks passed it seemed to her that the time she spent apart from Bake was time wasted, a dull passing of hours without meaning.

She went to the big public library at the corner of Michigan and Washington, and spent hours reading the books Bake talked about. Only the things that had some bearing on her relationship with Bake held any meaning. Only the hours that pointed to their next meeting had promise.

It was best when they met at the apartment. Once she got up the steps and inside the building she could fall into Bake's welcoming arms and forget all the emptiness since their last time together. But she gathered up crumbs of companionship too—the minutes they spent walking together, the after-class drink had become a ritual.

If it meant as much to Bake, she never said so. Gradually, as thought testing Frances's ability to enter into her life, she began to include Frances in her plans. She arranged for her to meet other friends, and told her small things—trivial in themselves but important because they helped to fill in the years they had spent apart—about her own life. Gradually, Frances came to see that another world lay all around her, whose existence she had never even suspected.

7 WHERE DO YOU THINK YOU'RE GOING?"
Frances paused with her hand on the doorknob. "A girl I know is having party. Any objections?"

"You're certianly leading a social life these days," Bill said. He laid his morning paper, still folded on the coffee table. His eyes rested on her—accusingly, or only questioningly? "How come?"

She smoothed her hair back nervously. "After all, you're hardly ever home anymore. You don't expect me to sit home alone evening after evening, do you?"

"I go out on business. I'm beating my brains out to earn a living for you and Bob, and you damn well know it. There's nothing I'd like better than a chance to stay home with my family once in a while."

"Is that why you play golf every Sunday?"

He ignored that. "If I didn't know better, I'd think you were running around with some other guy."

"Well, I'm not. I haven't got time to stand here and argue, either. I have a right to some friends of my own."

"You might try being decent to my friends for a change. You were snooty to Jack Flanagan again last night."

"I'm getting damn tired of having Jack Flanagan pinch me on the fanny every chance he gets," Frances said coldly. "I don't mind your eyes falling out of their sockets every time Betty leans over in those low-cut necklines of hers, but I don't care for that sort of thing myself." She pulled the front door open.

"This isn't like you."

"Maybe you don't know me very well. You're never home." She was rather proud of herself for keeping her voice so calm, considering the way her knees were shaking.

There were six or seven people in Bake's small apartment when she got there. The air was soft with smoke and loud with hi-fi blues. Frances made her way through the familiar rooms, trying not to feel that the guests were intruders, not to wish that they would all go home and leave her alone with Bake. She took off her coat and added it to the pile on the bed, reddened her lips, and smoothed her hair, pleased that she looked pretty. In the mirror she saw Bake come into the bedroom, closing the door tightly behind her.

"Hi," she said, sounding amused. "It's turning out to be quite a brawl. Are you staying afterward?"

"I can't. Bill made a fuss about my coming at all." She capped her lipstick and dropped it in her purse. "It's the first time he's ever said anything."

"You shouldn't have told him you were going out."

"Oh, hell, he's all settled down for a quiet evening at home. I don't know what got into him."

"He doesn't suspect anything, does he?"

"I don't think so. He accused me of being interested in another man," Frances said, giggling suddenly, "but I don't think he meant it. He was just peeved and wanted to hurt my feelings."

Bake lit a cigarette. She broke the match in two and flipped it at the corner wastebasket. "It's too bad you have to take him into consideration at all—and Bob too. I haven't anything against Bob, I'm sure he's a nice kid, but no adolescent really needs a mother. You're just a handy source of food and spending money to him."

Frances thought, I ought to resent that. I love Bob, he's my child. I'm sure he loves me too. Still, it's true that they start to make the real breakaway around this age.

She said stiffly, "Let's forget about it. Who's here?"

"Theresa and Kitty, Kay and Jane, Patsy and Barbara." Bake paused to count. "I've asked Lissa and Jo, but they've had a big fight and Jo moved out, bag and baggage. There's somebody else, of course. Lissa came alone. I'd just as soon she hadn't."

"Why not?"

"She likes you."

"You don't need to lose any sleep over that."

Frances was silent. The last time she had stayed after a party, it was to put a tangle-footed and incoherent Bake to bed. Bake caught her thought as she so often did.

"I'm sorry about that, darling. I won't drink so much tonight."

"What I hated about it," Frances said in a small hard voice, "was that Bill was awake when I got home. He wanted to make love to me—for a change."

"My God, Frankie."

"Well, what could I do? He's my husband."

Bake snapped off the bedroom light. In the half-dark, she caught Frances's arm in her two hands and shook her. "Did you like it?"

"I hated it."

But that wasn't the whole truth, she thought as she made her way back to the living room and took the glass Pat handed her. There had been a fluttering of response, the more insistent because she had tried to deny it. Even though she tried to lie unmoving and unfeeling until it was over, thinking about something else, it was one of the few times when she caught a glimmering of what the stories and poems were about. A dozen times, maybe, in sixteen years.

Afterward, lying beside a Bill oddly spent and gentle, more like the young husband of their early days than she had seen him for a long time, she had to fight back a wave of tenderness that threatened to engulf her. She had been short tempered with him ever since, in an effort to dispel that guilty tenderness, since it separated her somehow from Bake.

It's all her fault, she thought. If I hadn't had to go home all keyed up and unsatisfied . . .

This party was going to be like a dozen others she had gone to. Lots of talk, some music, a great deal to drink. All of Bake's friends drank more than she was used to—but so did all of Bill's friends. Alcohol seemed to be the solvent in which all differences of personality, background, and opinion were lost, so that people could endure being together. She walked through the living room, saying hello. She knew the girls now, all but one—the sulky brunette, not more than eighteen, sitting alone in front of the fireplace, who she supposed was Lissa. She shivered, feeling a real sympathy for the girl. God, suppose Bake ever left me, she thought.

Her first impulse was to sit down beside Lissa and try to distract the child from her troubles, but Bake was watching closely. She took her drink and went to sit with Kay and Pat, who were trading notes on their problems with the public school system.

Being with these women always made Frances miserably conscious that she was a housewife, without status in the world of earners. Barbara and Theresa held office jobs in the Loop; they were two digits in the crowds of young women who took the subway to work every morning. Jane was with an ad agency and had to spend most of her salary on clothes and beauty parlors. Tonight, as a reaction from the chic imposed on her by her job, she wore pedal pushers and moccasins, but her long nails were enameled silver-pink and her hairdo was elaborate. Kitty looked exactly what she was: an unmarried librarian of thirty-five: shrewd, sensible, and competent.

Until a few months ago, Frances might have sat next to any of them at a drugstore lunch counter without suspecting that any part of their lives was not open to scrutiny. She had heard a great deal about the telltale marks of the lesbian—mannish walk, severe dress, deep voice, short hair. All of these girls looked and acted exactly like any other youngish career woman. Lately she had been looking curiously at other women on the street and in the classroom, behind the counters of stores, and at restaurant tables, wondering which of them belonged to this world within a world whose existence she had not even suspected till now. There was absolutely no way to tell.

"Frankie, wake up, this is the third time I've spoken to you."

Frances blinked. "I'm sorry, I was just thinking what a good-looking crowd this is."

"Conventional looking, you mean." Jane smoothed down her pedal pushers, a gesture she had acquired from wearing sheath dresses. "What did you expect, a lot of butches?"

"Well—"

"There are some, you know. You'll see, if we go pub crawling after a while."

Bake asked, "Who's going pub crawling?"

"All of us, after you kick us out."

"After the booze is gone you mean," Pat suggested.

"I'll go too," Bake said, "if it will get you out of here any sooner."

Frances laughed. But there was a restless feeling in the room tonight that neither music nor liquor could dispel. She wanted to be alone with Bake, not only for the excitement and fulfillment of love but to talk. I'm not a party girl, she admitted, recognizing the onset of boredom that always overcame her when Bill persuaded her to go to a dance party or a bridge party. She looked around, but Bake was being a hostess, urging drinks and sandwiches on people.

"I'll go too," she said, taking a third martini.

It became evident after a while that the idea was growing. Maybe it was the tang of spring in the air, rising above the exhaust fumes and the varied smells of city life. Maybe it was the unrest fostered by the swollen eyes and drawn face of Lissa, who sat drinking steadily and silently. At last Kay said, "Well are we going slumming or are we not?" and there was a gradual gathering up of handbags and jackets. Bake snapped off the lights and replenished her supply of cigarettes and kitchen matches. "Going along, Frankie? You don't need your coat, you can pick it up later."

Lissa said in a low voice, going downstairs beside her, "I met you somewhere, didn't I?"

Pat said, "She's Bake's girl."

"Oh."

"Come on, Frankie, ride with us."

She looked around for Bake, who was backing out her own car. "Okay. Where are we goin?"

"Wherever Bake wants to go, I guess. It's her party. Besides, she knows all the places."

Lissa asked, "Have you been with Bake very long?"

"About five months."

"I was with Jo a year and a half."

Jane said, "For God's sake, baby, stop thinking about Jo. She'll come back."

"No, she won't. She's got somebody else."

"Look, kid, we've all been through it. You'll feel better pretty soon."

"I want to die," Lissa said. Her pretty, childish face puckered into a new burst of crying.

Jane gave Frances a look that said plainly, never mind, there's nothing to do for the poor kid. They were silent. Frances thought, will Bake and I separate some day, too? Is it impossible to stay together and go on loving?

She asked timidly, "How long have you been with Kay?"

"Fourteen months. Let's see—it'll be fifteen months next Wednesday." She turned the heavy silver ring she wore on her engagement finger. "We gave each other these on our first anniversary."

"And before that?"

"I don't know about Kay. She came from out on the Coast somewhere. But of course you know I used to—" She stopped suddenly, looking sharply at Frances.

"What?"

"Nothing."

Frances was silent. It was the first time she had thought about the future, and the picture was disquieting.

Karla's, where they rejoined the people from the other car, was a basement place on the near North Side, flanked by apartment buildings and lighted by a dim red neon sign. Frances had gone with Bake to three or four similar places, just outside the business district, but she still felt that there was something a little sinister about them.

She followed Jane down a flight of steps, paid her dollar admission, and helped group chairs around a too-small table so the nine of them could sit together. An awkward number. Here, as in the heterosexual world, where she lived with Bill, the animals came in two by two. She touched Bake's shoulder lightly as they took their places.

Bake ordered drinks all around. She had already had too much, Frances thought; her walk and speech were all right, but she had the shrewd narrow-eyed look with which she barricaded herself when she was beginning to feel her liquor.

Frances said, low, "Don't take anymore."

"Why not, for Christ's sake?"

"You've had enough."

Bake scowled. "Oh, all right. Dance?"

It still felt odd to be dancing with another woman. More than any other single thing, the sight of girls dancing together, which had reminded her of a high school gym class the first time she saw it, made her feel how far she had come from the world of conventional man-woman relationships. She went into Bake's arms feeling that this embrace, rather than the one they shared when they were alone, was unnatural. Yet there were only women in this place, some of them in dresses, some in the Ivy League shirts and tight pedal pushers you saw everywhere, a few in obviously masculine garb. Jane and Kay went by, cheek to cheek, and then little Lissa with a stranger. Bake waved at a girl with startling red hair, cut short and tightly curled.

"That's Cathleen Archer. She used to go with Barby."

"It makes me feel funny when you talk like that."

"Look, baby, nothing's permanent. How many married couples do you know that are still in love after, say, two or three years?"

Bake's hand was reassuring warmth against her back. She shut her eyes and let the jukebox music, strongly accented, take over.

"Wake up," Bake said. "We're going on to someplace more interesting.

8

HOW ABOUT ANOTHER DRINK ALL AROUND?"

Frances shook her head. Motion made it ache and she stopped. "Had too much now," she said owlishly.

"The hell I have."

"Somebody has to drive."

Bake thought this over, leaning against the bar. "Okay. You're all wrong, but I'm not going to argue with you. If you want me to drive, I'll drive. Lissa, drink?"

"I feel so terrible," Lissa whispered. She had started crying again, and her eyes were swollen almost shut. "What difference does it make?"

"That's the spirit," the girl standing beside her said. She wore the heavy sweater and fly-front jeans that were regulation here; her hair was cut short and slicked down. "You got trouble, baby?"

"Her girl left her," Jane said sadly.

"Poor kid. Listen, why don't you come home with me? I got a double bed. You could get a good night's sleep."

"I bet," Jane said. "Goddamn butch."

Kay said urgently, "What's it to you? That's what makes me so angry, darling. It happens every time. Every time I ask you to be nice to some little tramp, just out of politeness, you go overboard. What do you care where she goes or who she goes with?"

"She's just a child," Jane said with a drunken dignity. She pushed her hair back to give Kay the full benefit of a cold look. "An innocent little child. Somebody has to take care of her."

"Look, you take care of me. Just concentrate on that. You don't need to worry about anybody else."

She sounded like Bill. Frances said, "Oh, my God, what time is it?"

Bake squinted at her watch. "Twenty past two. That can't be right, can it?"

"I have to go home."

"But you're supposed to go home with me," Bake said in a hurt voice. "You promised."

"Just for a little while then."

Bill would be sound asleep by this time. Or would he? She had a crazy mental image of him still sitting in the armchair where she had left him, his feet propped on the hassock watching the door accusingly above yesterday morning's *Tribune*. Bill Ollenfield, a model of domestic virtue and handyman around the house—once every six months. Why did he have to pick a night when she had a date? Was she supposed to sit around the house night after night, waiting for him to get tired of his drinking and whoring customers and come home to her loving arms?

Or maybe he was lying tense and wide awake as she had done so often, watching the lights of passing cars sweep across the bedroom wall and waiting for the sound of her step on the stairs. She giggled.

"Sauce for the gander," she said.

"Right, right," Jane said, not knowing or caring what she was talking about.

Bake said, "Who's that girl in the green dress? The one that just came in? I'd swear I know her from someplace."

Frances followed her gaze to the doorway, where a party of three men and three young girls stood, looking around curiously. "Goddamn tourists," the girl beside Lissa said. "Out to get a great big thrill looking at the queers." She tipped her glass.

"I've seen her too. On campus, I think."

"That's great," Bake said. "Just great." She laid a shaky hand on Frances arm. "Come on, let's go home. I'm tired."

The girl in green stared at them as they left, and then laughed.

It was a mean laugh. It chilled Frances. She pushed her way out behind Bake. The crowd had thinned. There were half a dozen parties like their own, trying to spin the evening's festivity out to breakfast time, and three or four couples sitting drink sodden and silent at small tables; also a few single women, mostly middle aged, cruising. There were five or six butches waiting for their girls to get through work.

Jane said, "Crummy bunch, huh?"

Kay shrugged.

"There aren't any sunrises in this town," Frances complained. She found the car keys in Bake's pocket, since Bake seemed unable to locate them, and handed them to her. "We had sunrises at home. Here the sky keeps getting lighter, and pretty soon it's time to get up." The eastern sky was changing from lead gray. She felt very sad.

"Why do I do these things? Why do you let me?" Bake backed out expertly. The street was deserted except for a cruising taxi and a prowl car. "God, that's a grim place. I don't know why we went there."

"It seemed like a good idea at the time."

"A good expensive idea. I was going to buy that South American pottery this week."

"We spend too much on booze."

"You're telling me."

The dawn air was cold. Frances shivered. She put her hand in the other girl's jacket pocket. "I don't want to go home Bake."

"I thought you were coming home with me. That was the idea in the first place."

Frances considered. If she went home now it would mean another fight. If Bill was asleep when she got in, her arrival would almost certainly wake him and he would raise hell. (Not without reason, she admitted, feeling herself crumpled and dim eyed.) On the other hand, if she waited until he had left for the office it would postpone the fight until evening and by that time it would have lost vitality.

Neither anger nor anxiety would keep young Mr. Ollenfield, sales manager for Plastic Playthings, from being at his desk by nine o'clock, teeth brushed, suit pressed, shoes shined, hair combed. Because young Mr. Ollenfield was going to get ahead in the world or know the reason why; and after all, what's a wife compared to a bigger expense account and money in the bank?

She was too tired and confused to explain all this to Bake. She said, "Oh, let him sleep with his sales reports."

"But baby, why do you keep worrying about the man? He's old enough to cook his own breakfast. I hope it gives him ulcers."

I'm turning into the kind of woman who stays out all night, Frances thought. A tramp. The perpetual feeling of guilt that lived in the back of her mind uncoiled and stirred, ready to sting. She summoned up all her resentment against Bill—after all, hadn't he stayed out plenty of nights, doing God knows what? Doing plenty, I'll bet, she thought defensively. She put her hand on Bake's knee, anxious to feel the solidarity, the reality of her.

"Okay, do we have any coffee?"

The apartment was a mess. Bake drifted around, still a little fuzzy, emptying ashtrays, opening windows, carrying glasses into the kitchen. "God, I'm tired."

"Come to bed, I'll let you sleep—if that's what you want."

"Is it what you want?"

Frances's mouth curled into an unwilling smile. "Not exactly."

Bake yawned widely, unzipping her pedal pushers and letting them fall to the floor. "It wouldn't have to be like this," she said, her voice muffled by the shirt she was pulling over her head. "You wouldn't have to be so rushed, you know. You could move in here."

"But how?" The obligations of her life loomed solid and implacable—Bill, Bob, the house. She stared at Bake.

"Easy. Pack up your stuff and move out."

"I couldn't do that."

"All right, don't. It's up to you."

"But how could I?"

"It's been done before. Kay was married, you know. She

divorced her husband to live with Jane. She was married to Carlton Schofield, the atomic scientist."

Frances felt a surge of sympathy for Kay, and some envy. "What would I live on?"

"Oh hell, you can always get a job. I can get you a job, if that's all that's worrying you." Bake stood naked in the half-light from the shuttered window, her head bent thoughtfully. "There are plenty of jobs. You could work in an office."

"I'd like to go to work anyway. It would be nice to have some money of my own, not have to ask Bill for every penny. Not that he minds, only—"

"Only you feel like a whore."

"Well, yes, I do." She shook her head. "I can't do it though." Bake shrugged. "It's up to you. Are you coming to bed or not?"

This is silly, Frances thought. Their argument was taking on the familiar pattern of a married quarrel, in the familiar setting of getting ready for bed. She and Bill had bickered like this, tired and edgy after an evening out: had tried and failed to make up for it with physical closeness. It occurred to her suddenly that she would like to skip the next part of the night and simply go to sleep in Bake's arms. But this is the way I used to feel with Bill, she thought, aghast. She stripped off her clothes and got into bed, sighing a little.

Later Frances lay in a relaxed half doze, watching the oblong of the window lighten. It would be wonderful to have a job, to be one of the fast-walking girls she saw downtown, going to a desk job every morning. Most wonderful of all to live in this apartment with Bake, sharing their breakfast over two propped-up books and having plenty of time to talk. Lately their scattered hours together had been invaded by too many people, their companionship diluted by too much drinking. They were wasting time and spending too much money—Bake's money, since Frances had none of her own.

"I'm tired of being a freeloader," she said.

Bake rolled over. "Huh?"

Frances moved closer to her, seeking comfort in contact.

There was Bob. For fifteen years her days had been shaped to his needs. She might leave Bill—but not her son, no. Not even now, when he was outgrowing her.

"Matter, baby?"

"Ssh, go to sleep."

Perhaps she could get a job, though. That would give her some money of her own, and make it easier to stay downtown on the evenings she spent with Bake. As things stood, every move she made laid her open to suspicion.

She was getting warm and drowsy. She could feel her arms and legs relax. I'll decide tomorrow, she thought, shutting her eyes and falling asleep with her hand against Bake's breast.

9 IT SEEMED TO FRANCES, ALL WINTER, THAT SHE WAS warm for the first time in her life. Warm and at home, solidly and actually when she was with Bake, in retrospect or anticipation when they were apart.

It was foolish, it was fantastic, because the house on the South Side, for example, had a perfectly good gas furnace—indeed, the first thing Bill did when he came in after work was to throw the windows open and "get some fresh air in here," while she shivered. But she felt that some residue of chill, lingering in the center of her bones, was melted now for the first time. I've thawed out, she decided solemnly, curled up on Bake's sofa, listening to the rattling of dishes as Bake cooked dinner, while she (presumably) took a nap because she had a sniffly cold.

She had known real, physical cold, of course. The winter she was thirteen, when they chopped up the doors for firewood because the mine was on strike and there was no money for food, much less fuel. Even reading didn't help. Your fingers got stiff holding the book, and the chill crept down between your scrunched-together shoulders and up your stockinged legs. Frankie had been hungry before, plenty of times, when the miners were out or Pa spent all his pay on drinks. But this was worse than being hungry.

"I should have married one of the neighbor boys at home," Ma once said. "A farmer can always raise something to eat." Pa gave her a sour look. "For Christ's sake shut up and quit bawling. You ain't never starved yet."

"Darrell did."

Frankie, hanging around the kitchen door, began to whimper. She had heard all she wanted to hear about Darrell, who just sort of dwindled away because Ma didn't have any milk for him and there was no money to buy groceries. The other kids were too little to understand what Ma's bulging apron meant. Frankie was a little vague on the details herself, but she knew there was going to be another baby soon—and there was no money this time either, and the house was nightmare cold.

"I'll go out after dark and rob a vein," Pa said, surly.

"With company guards all over the place?"

The MacAllister boy, shot down by the company police, lay in his mother's frigid front room with the cheekbones cutting through the wasting flesh and the stink of his gangrened wound filling the house. The company doctor didn't bother with strikers, especially if they were known to carry union cards.

"Dirty Sonsabitches," Pa said. "Shoot down their own mothers, company police would. A decent man wouldn't give them the time of day. A decent man would kill the bastards."

Frances said nothing. She had seen Bob MacAllister's own cousin Loren at the pit mouth, a boy who had gone fishing with the neighborhood kids a couple of summers before, beefy now with good food and armed with a police revolver. Had wondered if he was the one who fired the shot that pitched Bob on his face in the dirt.

Ma shook the last of the flour into the pan and turned the sack inside out. "Seems like I could stand it if I could get warmed up," she said. "Just for a minute even."

Pa stood up. He was stooped from years of hard work and his dark thick hair was going gray, but he was still a big man, with iron muscles in his arms and shoulders, "I'll warm you up. Lorena, fetch me the ax."

So the doors came down, not neatly but with ragged blows

of the old ax, and were hacked into kindling. Pa stuffed the cookstove and shook the coal-oil can hopefully, although they hadn't lit the lamp for more than a week. Then he ripped pages out of Frankie's geography book, and her heart tore across like paper.

But she stood up close to the stove with the others when the orange flames began to lick up and the first warmth stole out into the cold room. She held Delano up to see the red light flicker around the stovelids, and he forgot his sore chapped bottom and the hunger sores at the corners of his mouth, and held his hands out to the light. Wonderful warmth—even Ma smiled, feeling her stiffness melt away and her long-carried dread lighten.

Frances, lying on Bake's sofa, sighed. And then tensed again, remembering that night when she lay awake and heard from behind the gaping doorway of her parents' bedroom the rise and fall of creaking springs, the muffled masculine whisper and the other, higher-pitched protest that she had been hearing from behind the closed door all her life. Only now there was no door to close. Lying on the front room cot that had been all hers since Wanda married, she could see as well as hear. Moonlight came in the uncurtained window and lay across the patchwork quilt. Pretty soon the quilt slipped off, and the moonlight showed her the confused shape of two people merged into one. She was afraid and ashamed to look and unable to stop looking.

This was marriage, then. She had guessed at it last summer, when she came upon her sister Wanda and Chris Hollister in the woods, before they were married. But they were dressed, or partly so, and when they saw her standing there, Wanda smoothed down her skirt and Chris ran to hide behind a tree. So she hadn't been sure, had tried to fill in the gaps and empty places from her imagination.

"Oh God, Joe, you're killing me. It's too near my time."

A bass growl. The springs creaked faster and faster.

Frances squeezed her eyes shut. Hurry up, she begged silently. Hurry up and get it over with.

The sight of Wanda, the next day, sickened her even more. Married at fifteen and already pregnant with her first baby,

Wanda had taken on the look of the older woman, at once resentful and smug. Chris's widowed mother, lucky to be on home relief, had sent over a little brown paper sack of wheat and flour and one of dried prunes, and Wanda dropped them on the table and sat down heavily.

"God my back aches."

Frankie stood beside the oilcloth-covered table, turning the little sack of prunes over and over in her hand. "Sis, do you like it—being married?"

"It's all right, I guess. Sure, isn't much like you think it'll be." Wanda looked at her curiously. "What are you so interested for, all of a sudden?"

"I was thinking about Ma. Seems like she's never had anything but kids and hard work."

Wanda said, "Men's all alike, near about."

Frankie bent her head to read the fine printing on the prune bag. "I don't ever aim to get married."

"I used to say that too," Wanda laughed harshly. "Wait till the love bug bites you."

The gray of Frankie's eyes deepened, under the fine brows that were her only beauty. "I'm going to be a schoolteacher like Ma was, only I'm going to stay one."

"An old-maid schoolteacher?"

"Sooner be an old maid than have a baby every year."

Wanda sighed, cradling her bulge against the edge of the table. "Stay away from the men, then. Frankie, it's like an icebox in here."

Frances, remembering the skinny scab-kneed little girl she had been, shivered. She opened her eyes and looked at the embers in Bake's fireplace, glowing softly through a fine coating of ashes. "It's nice and warm in here," she said softly.

"It better be. I've got the gas bills to prove it." Bake appeared in the doorway, a smudge of flour on her check. "You're supposed to be asleep."

Frances blinked, "I hate to waste the time. We hardly even get a whole day."

Bake grinned. "So rest. You'll be glad later."

Frances sighed. It was no use. She could never make anybody understand how wonderful it was to be warm clear through. Nobody else could possibly know.

She got up, a little groggily, and followed Bake into the kitchen. She stood, leaning against the doorframe, watching Bake as she opened the oven door and slid a pan in. This was a different Bake, her very own, no kin to the girl striding along against the wind or the girl reaching out in bed. Her heart warmed—all the way through.

"What's the matter, baby?"

"You know something?"

"Sure." Bake wiped her hands on the dishtowel. "Me too."

10

"THIS IS GOING TO BE A REAL VACATION," BAKE said. Her face glowed as it always did when she was describing some project of her own devising. "It's our anniversary. We've been together two years."

"Good God," Jane said, "that set some kind of record. Of course Kay and I have been together almost four, but that's different."

"Yes," Bake said with something steely and ominous in her voice, "I know damn well—"

Lissa cut in, "Are you going to have a party? I love parties."

"Nope. We're going on a trip, a week or maybe two weeks if Frankie can get her vacation now. I've been thinking about Quebec, French Canada."

"Cold there this time of year," Jane said, breaking her Ry-Krisp and looking at it distastefully.

Frances said, "But Bake!"

Polly said maliciously, "Frances doesn't sound so enthusiastic. Maybe she isn't as crazy about sub-zero weather as you are."

"It isn't that," Frances said, troubled. "I'd love to go. Only I didn't plan on being gone so long during the school year."

"I suppose your child goes to camp in the summer," Polly

said dryly. "How old is he now, old enough to wash his own neck and ears?"

"Seventeen. I know it sounds foolish, he's really old enough to take care of himself. But I don't like to leave him."

"The old maternal instinct. I use mine all up on Lissa, the big baby."

Lissa widened her eyes. "But Polly honey, I need to be taken care of."

"Sometimes I think both of those girls are feeble minded." Bake said sharply when Polly had paid the waiter and left, with Lissa trailing along. "I can't understand Polly. She used to be such an intelligent girl. It isn't in that stupid little bitch of a Lissa to be faithful to anybody." She took the slip the waiter handed her and sat moodily studying it. "Goddamn it, we can't even have a quiet meal together anymore. Everybody has to come bursting in."

Frances managed not to point out that the other three had been seated on the other side of the room until Bake called them over. There was no point in arguing with her when she was in this mood, especially after a couple of drinks. Bake's plans began to take on substance only after she had shared them with somebody else—she had to talk herself into things.

Jane said, "Looks like it's time for me to go. I'll see you girls later." And left.

Frances said again, urgently. "But Bake."

"What?"

"You know I can't get away for two weeks just now. Or a week, even. I thought maybe we could go somewhere for a weekend."

"Look, you went without a vacation all last summer when everybody else was going off on cruises and what not. You've got all that time stacked up. There's absolutely no reason why we can't go to Canada for a couple of weeks—or a month if we feel like it. Ski in the Laurentians, see the old French farms where they use the bullock carts—"

"That's not it."

Bake dropped a handful of change on the cashier's desk, and held the door open for her. "Look, that boy of yours is a senior in high school. He'll go away to college next year—I suppose Bill's set on an eastern school for him? Okay, nobody's going to wipe his nose for him then. Don't you think it's about time you cut the apron strings?"

"Bill would make a terrible fuss."

"Bill doesn't need you either, for heaven's sake. He needs somebody who will send his suits to the cleaner and not care how late he stays out or how many secretaries he sleeps with, just so he brings home the paycheck. The guys Bill runs around with could trade wives blindfolded and never notice any difference. You're wasting your life."

Frances said slowly, "Sometimes I think Bill knows. About us, I mean."

"Then what have you got to lose? Just tell him you're leaving."

Frances picked her way across the slush-slippery intersection, keeping a weary eye out for taxis. It was an overcast day, gray and windy. Bake slipped a hand under her elbow, a rare gesture. Her usual public behavior was impersonal to the point of being curt.

"Remember our first day? It wasn't much like this."

Frances's eyes misted. "No, it wasn't."

"Damn it, you sound like you were reading the obituary page. There's no reason it can't stay good. You're not the first person to make a stupid marriage and you wouldn't be the first person to get out of one, either. Sometimes I think you're simply too lazy."

"I keep telling myself."

"As far as Bill's concerned," Bake said coldly, "he's nothing but a Babbitt. I don't care how noble and idealistic he was when you married him, he doesn't know the first thing about you after—what is it, eighteen, nineteen years? I knew you better after eighteen minutes. In another ten years he'll have a paunch, a bald spot, and an ulcer, and it'll be like living with

The Wall Street Journal." She looked shrewdly at Frances. "In another ten years Bob will be married and have a couple of kids, too. Then what have you got to live for?"

"Oh God, you make it sound so horrible. Don't you suppose I've thought about all that?"

"If you didn't have to rush home from the office and cook dinner, you could take some evening courses and finish your degree work. I've always been sorry you dropped out when you went to work."

"What else could I do?"

"Nothing, I guess, as long as you're determined to be a household drudge."

"I'd have left anyway, after what that awful girl said to me in the washroom."

Bake shrugged. "That's a chance you take. It would have been the same thing if she saw you out with a man—well, no, not quite the same, but she was only kidding. You shouldn't have taken it so seriously."

"She wasn't kidding."

"Then you shouldn't have denied it."

Frances was silent. They reached her office building, tall, many-windowed, impersonal. "All right," she said abruptly, "I'll do it."

"What, go to Quebec with me?"

"That too. But I mean, I'll leave Bill." She swallowed hard. "I can't tell him till next week though; he has his pre-Christmas convention coming up."

"You're scared to tell him."

"Yes, I am. But I will, as soon as the convention is over. That's a promise."

"Good girl. That gives me time to scout around and find a good lawyer. In this state you have to prove cruelty or infidelity, I think. You might ask Kay—she's been divorced."

"I like Kay."

"So does Jane," Bake said dryly. "Maybe we better postpone the trip, after all. If it got back to Bill, he might file a countersuit or something. We don't want anything to keep your decree from coming through. And God knows," Bake said, "we don't want any publicity."

"It sounds so messy."

"Not with a good lawyer. Look, baby, I'm late for an appointment. We'll talk it over tonight, shall we? We'll get everything settled and then go on a real binge, just the two of us."

"What, no Jane?"

"Don't be bitchy. You know Jane's an old friend."

Frances hesitated. "Okay. I'll be down around eight."

The glow of determination ebbed away as she rang for the elevator and then stood waiting, going over her problem for the hundredth time. There isn't any good solution, she thought, feeling a little sick as the elevator door slid shut and the floors slid past. There just isn't any way out of this. No matter what I do, it's all wrong.

She hung her coat on the rack in the office washroom and absentmindedly opened the first of her salesmen's reports. I've promised, she reminded herself unhappily. I can't back down now.

She felt confused and depressed.

As for the job, it was just a job. For the first few weeks it had been exciting to come to the Loop every morning, feeling herself part of the crowd that poured into the packed blocks between Michigan and Clark, Van Buren and Lake. Then the glamour wore thin and figuring commissions on insurance policies became no more exciting than washing dishes. Only the freedom that went with earning money—even though most of it went for clothes, lunches, and bus fares—and the necessity to prove some degree of independence, kept her at her desk.

Two years of it, she thought. Two long years of hurrying to get my desk cleared by five thirty so I can get home and wash the breakfast dishes. Then Bill's at a committee meeting or a business dinner, or out on the town with a customer, and Bob has something on at school. And me with nothing to look forward to but social security when I'm sixty-five, if I live that long.

She thought as she had thought almost every day for the last two years what it would mean to live with Bake. I'll do it, she promised herself. I won't back down this time.

But she was glad that she didn't have to break the news to Bill for a few days.

11 MOM?" THAT WAS BOB IN THE LIVING ROOM, probably home for a supper after all. The slam of the front door reverberated through the house. Frances reached for the hand lotion, trying to keep her voice level, and wondering what she could fix for him to eat. "In the kitchen, son."

He looked like his father, a tall sturdy man whose breadth filled the kitchen doorway. Frances smiled mechanically. Then she saw that he wasn't alone. He had a girl with him, a slim splinter of a girl with smooth dark hair and curving black eyebrows. He pulled her into the room after him. "Mom, this is Mary Congdon."

Frances said something polite. Since he was fourteen he had been bringing home girls—blondes, brunettes, redheads and some who got their coloring out of a bottle and changed it every week. Kids started dating now before they were out of eight grade, and all of the girls were smart looking and self-possessed, but they all looked alike to an adult. Sometimes she wondered how Bob told them apart.

This one was different. Young as she was, surely no more than seventeen, she had a mature quality that the others lacked. Or maybe it was the expression on Bob's face that made the difference. His mother caught her breath, watching him. That mixture of tenderness, amusement, and hunger—it was the look of a man in love. And the girl had the quiet awareness of a loved woman, for whom all things are intensified.

I'm imaging things, she told herself crossly. Aloud she said, "I have to go out in an hour or so, but wouldn't you youngsters like something to eat?"

Bob looked embarrassed. The girl said in a low composed

53

voice, "Thank you, but we have a date. Bob's been wanting me to meet you, and I thought—you see, he had to come home and change anyway—"

Frances said more cordially, "Well, I'm glad you did. You must come and have dinner with us. Maybe Sunday?" Then she remembered that she was going to break the news to Bill on Sunday. I won't be seeing Bob anymore unless I call up and make an appointment with him. Do they let the mother have visiting privileges, if the father has custody?

Nonsense, Bob's almost eighteen. He makes his own decisions. She glanced at him covertly, seeing him with that man look on his face, and desolation settled down over her. The apron strings were snapped now, sure enough.

She became aware of the silence that had settled down. Bob said gruffly, "Well, come on," and the girl followed him out of the kitchen, turning back to offer Frances a sweet, apologetic smile. She had on heels and nylons: a formal date, then. Frances wondered fleetingly where they were going. Then her own problems came rushing back. She snapped off the kitchen light and went upstairs, feeling tired and shopworn, to dress for an evening on the town with Bake.

She didn't much care for the places Bake and her crowd frequented, places where women danced together and the only men were blatant queers or gawking sightseers from out of town. Bake knew all sorts of interesting people: painters, writers, newspapermen, publishers, corporation lawyers, atomic scientists, museum curators. Because of her job she had an entree to supper clubs and restaurants that were mentioned in smart magazines. But when she was in the mood for relaxation she liked to go to Karla's, the Squared Circle, the Gay Eighties. Special clientele, Frances thought wryly. Too special. She wasn't ashamed of loving Bake, but she didn't want to be classified with the couples she had seen in the Gay Eighties, looking into each other's eyes, holding hands under the table. Or with the lonely haunted women who drifted in after midnight, ordered drink after drink and scanned the room for possible pickups.

When they were at the apartment, she could forget her qualms in Bake's arms. But tonight they met downtown, on a busy street corner. Frances gathered up her courage. "Bake, why don't we go straight to your place? I'd like us to be alone for once."

"Would you, darling?" Bake had already had a couple of drinks. She smiled. "I tell you what, we'll go over to Karla's and have just one. Then we'll go right home."

"Not Karla's. It's so tacky."

Bake's eyes narrowed. "If the places I like aren't good enough for you—

"I didn't mean that." It was no good reasoning with Bake: Frances had seen her in this mood before. She slipped her arm through Bake's, resolving to try to get her home early. "Taxi?"

"Certainly. We're celebrating, aren't we?"

Karla's was jammed. Jukebox blasting, waitress pushing and twisting to make a path among the small tightly crowded tables, people talking loudly to be heard above the music. Bake headed straight for the bar. A husky butch and her femme were just getting up to leave and Bake grabbed their stools.

"The joint's jumping," she said.

The bartender—Frances had seen her three or four times before she realized that Mickey was a girl—nodded. "Yeah, the word's getting around. Friday night too, that helps." She reached under the counter for clean glasses. "The usual?"

"Double. We're celebrating."

"I haven't seen you two in quite a while. Thought maybe you split up or something."

"Uh-uh. We're not going to split up, are we baby?"

Frances murmured, "I hope not."

"This girl's moving in with me." Bake chose her words with care, enunciating precisely. "Isn't that great? She's going to leave her dumb husband and come in with me. Smartest thing she ever did."

"Please Bake."

Bake slid one of the martinis her way. "To us."

Frances sipped her drink and fatigue and apprehension fell

away. The faint guilt that had nagged at her since the meeting with Bob's girl vanished. "I never used to drink at all," she said in wonder.

"You missed out on a good thing," Bake said. "Make us another, will you, Mickey?"

"Sure thing."

Frances couldn't remember why she had disliked Mickey so at first. She made a good-looking boy, solid and healthy. Only the slight swell under the pockets of her plaid shirt and something indefinable in her walk gave her away. Not more than twenty-five, she had rosy cheeks and smooth, dark hair; she managed the bar competently and seemed to be in charge whenever the gray-haired manager was out, which was most of the time. Of course I couldn't go for anybody like that, she defended herself. Bake's not queer, but I don't have to be narrow-minded about other people, do I?

She accepted her second double martini through a pleasant haze of goodwill.

Bake was sitting very erect, holding her glass carefully. She'll be alright, Frances reassured herself. Never shows it when she's had too much; I wouldn't know it myself if she didn't get so guarded.

She nudged Bake. "Please don't take anymore."

"It's all right, I won't pass out on you this time." She said to Mickey, laughing. "About the second time we were together I got plastered and went to sleep before I hit the pillow. She's never forgiven me."

"Dance?"

She turned. A tall, thin woman of her own age stood beside her, dangling a cigarette from her veined hand. Frances said uncertainly, "I don't think so, thanks."

"She doesn't want to dance with you," Bake said.

"That's up to her. Do you want to dance or not, honey?"

"Look," Bake said. "I told you she doesn't want to dance." She stood up. So did Frances. "Listen, Bake, let's go home now, I'm tired."

The thin woman looked Bake up and down, her eyebrows raised. "Are you married to the girl or something? I only asked her to dance."

Bake said between her teeth, "Will you go away?" She moved closer to the woman, who took an uncertain step backward and stood swaying a little on high heels. Oh God, Frances thought, she's loaded too.

Mickey said, "Break it up, kids. Let's be friends."

"Friends, hell," Bake said. "Get out of here, you bitch."

She laid her hand against the woman's flat chest and pushed. The other customer, caught off balance, went down gradually, like someone in a slow-motion film. There was a sickening thud as her head struck the edge of the bar.

A couple of girls near the door, the worse for drink, turned and took in the situation. The smaller of them began to babble. Her friends gripped her by the shoulders, pushed her through the entrance door and disappeared after her. Mickey grabbed the telephone from its little shelf under the bar and began to dial.

"Have the riot squad in here if we don't watch out," she said to nobody in particular. "Better let the boys on the beat bust it up."

Bake said, "Oh, God," and looked around wildly. Someone emptied a half-filled glass of water on the victim's face. She lay absolutely motionless.

"Out cold," Mickey said.

The whole thing had taken perhaps a minute, certainly not more than two. Half a dozen people at nearby tables had seen it, and sat staring. A buzz of talk rose and swelled. Frances looked at Bake, unbelieving. She opened her mouth but no sound came out. It was like a bad dream. Everything seemed suspended for a moment.

The jukebox clicked, changing records, and the oompah oompah of a polka filled the room.

Someone screamed. A high school girl in the rear of the room burst into loud hysterical sobs.

A group of customers got to their feet and headed for the door. Others, released by their movement, began milling around, trying to see what had happened.

Mickey began to pick up used glasses, keeping her eyes on the door.

Two uniformed policemen suddenly filled the doorway. Mickey said in a whisper, "Oh, those bitches." The few customers who were still dancing, unaware of what had happened, jerked to a standstill. Two girls in the far corner, who had been standing locked in each other's arms for the last five minutes, froze into immobility.

Frances's first reaction was one of pure unbelief. The men were so husky and ruddy, so masculine, that her eyes wouldn't accept them in this place. Then she realized, with a shock of awakening, that the two cops had already gone into action, as if this situation were routine. (Which of course it is, she reminded herself.) They were lining up the customers and herding them out of the door, single file. Ignoring complaints, feminine screams and muffled curses, they worked efficiently from table to table. As the taller of the men turned his back she saw that he wore a cartridge belt and a service revolver, an ugly snub-nosed thing—standard equipment for the city police, even traffic cops had them, but it had never occurred to her before that a policeman might actually shoot someone. Anyone. Her.

Her mouth was parched and tinny tasting. She retched dryly, then stiffened as the shorter officer stopped beside her.

"This the one who started it?"

She looked into his small eyes, uncomprehending. Mickey shook her head. "No, she's all right."

"I'm sorry, you'll have to come too. You," he said to Mickey, "stay till the ambulance gets here, will you?" I can't move the victim, she might be hurt bad." He gave Frances a hard look. "Come on, come on, what are you waiting for?"

Bake, of course. She realized, in stupid surprise, that Bake was nowhere in sight. She said, "Me?"

"Yeah, you."

She followed him on rubbery legs, numb and unbelieving.

The paddy wagon was backed up to the curb. A dozen specta-tors had already gathered on the sidewalk. "It's a raid."

"Sure, a lot of queers." "Somebody prob'ly pulled a knife, some of those babies are tough." A young girl, pregnant, cling-ing to her husband's arm, looked at Frances with curiosity and pity. Frances gave the look back, cold and hard.

The two cops herded them in, quietly and quickly, like farm-ers loading livestock. Frances, almost the last in, found stand-ing room between a small girl in her late teens and a sulky butch in denim pants and one gold hoop earring. Some of the women were stolid, some crying. One was giggling hysterically against her friend's shoulder.

She twisted to look, hungry for a glimpse of Bake's face, feeling that she could bear anything if Bake would only look at her and smile. But Bake was not there.

"One thing," the butch with the earring said matter-of-factly, "they don't generally search you on a morals charge." She pat-ted her skirt pocket. "Any of you fellows got any reefers, you better get rid of them on the way in, just the same. Some of those goddamn matrons got itchy fingers."

"In where?" her high school friend asked.

"Jail, stupid. The pokey. Did you think the mayor was hav-ing a reception for us, or something?"

I've been arrested, Frances told herself. The words had no meaning. She braced herself against the jolt as the vehicle started.

12

FRANCES'S MENTAL PICTURE OF PRISONS HAD been culled from the movies. Grim gray fortresses surrounded by high walls, on which armed guards were mounted with machine guns; circling searchlights; a con-crete yard where uniformed convicts marched silently under guard. Sing Sing, Alcatraz, Joliet.

The wagon jolted to a stop in front of a red brick structure, no bigger than a supermarket or a firehouse, indistinguishable from the other buildings on the block except for a small barred windows set high in the walls. The butch with the gold ear-ring caught Frances's look as she stepped down, a little stiffly because her legs were still cramped with fright.

"Precinct station, a hick dump. I'll be out of here before you can say scat."

"Wait till I get in touch with my lawyer!" The plump middle-aged woman beside Frances pulled her fur scarf closer around her throat, looking disdainfully at her fellow prisoners. "They can't do this to me."

"The hell they can't," the butch said.

"Quiet, please. No talking. Line up by twos."

The smell hit you as you went in, before you got a clear view of the room. Like the country courthouse back home: tobacco, sweat, plumbing Lysol. Frances followed the others into a large almost-bare room and stood waiting patiently for further instructions.

The taller cop slammed the door shut and lounged against it, looking bored. The girl with the earring said, "Might as well be comfortable. They take their good old easy time in this dump," and sat down, her feet apart.

There were wooden benches along the walls, some old-fashioned kitchen chairs, a few folding chairs. That was all. The walls were painted light green up to about eight feet and cream above, both colors dingy, the green, defaced at shoulder level by pencil scrawls and streaks of lipstick. The floor was littered with cigarette butts. In one corner a semi-partition hid the sight but not the smell of a lidless toilet and a small round washbasin, both badly in need of scouring, A metal wastebasket overflowed with crumpled paper towels, but the dispenser above the basket was empty.

"Crummy dump. You'd think they'd clean the can, anyhow."

"These dumb cops aren't used to anything better. Prob'ly live like this at home."

"The dumb matrons are the worst."

The woman unlocking the door looked angry. She also looked stupid. Middle-aged, thick-hipped; if she had worn a blue apron dress instead of the uniform of a police matron, Frances would have taken her for one of the women who come out after dark to clean office buildings. Her thick face was framed in a frizzy permanent. "I'll take your cigarettes and liquor. Any of you ladies got a switchblade on you?" Nobody answered. She ran her hands over the pockets of a girl who might have been a secretary or a saleswoman.

"Get your dirty hands off me before I hit you."

"That's no way to talk." But she stepped back.

The taller policeman, standing inside the door, said, "I thought you girls like to smooch each other."

"Anyhow, I've never been low enough to go out with a cop."

"Hush, Barby, or they'll never let you go."

"So what?"

"Names and addresses, please?"

"I want to call my lawyer!"

"Later. Give your correct names and addresses, please."

But most of the women were silent, from fear or caution. The ones with regular jobs in the straight world, Frances guessed—the ones who had the most to lose.

Bake's desertion stung like iodine on an open cut. I ought to be glad she isn't involved, Frances thought. The words had no meaning. All that mattered was that Bake was not there.

"Where's your girlfriend?"

"I was alone." The lie was automatic. She gave the name of a girl she had disliked in high school, and a made-up address. The matron wrote it down, without comment.

When she had gone out again, locking the door behind her, the girl with the gold earring moved over beside Frances. She didn't look sulky now but spunky, as if she had found something to fight for or, at least, somebody to fight with.

She said, "You were with the one that started it, weren't you?"

"Yes."

"What prob'ly happened, she got out through the washroom and down the alley."

"What happens now?"

"They call the families. Some of them will come around and bail the girls out. Might be twenty bucks, might be fifty, might be a hundred. Depends on a lot of things. The rest come to trial in a week or so."

"On what charge?"

Her new friend smiled ironically. "Oh—disturbing the peace or something. Legally they can't fine you till you're charged with something. But a trial's too much bother for the cops who made the pickup, they have to appear in court and all. So they let everybody out on bail." She looked around at her fellow prisoners. "Most of these babes will be out by tonight. They figure its better to pay than get their names in the paper and maybe lose their jobs."

"But a citizen has rights."

"Not if she's one of the girls. Don't you know how straight people feel about us? They got it fixed so you can't fight back."

It was full day now. The window squares were bright, striped with the black metal bars against the sun. A man in uniform came to the door and called a name. The high school girl who had been with the butch turned and gave her an imploring look, then followed him out.

"Christ," her friend said, "am I glad to see her go! My steady girl would kill me if she found out."

Others left one by one. Frances could visualize the whole thing: ringing phone, husband or father jumping up to answer, the search through drawers and pockets for money. (Would they take a check?) She was stubbornly glad she hadn't given Bill's name.

After a while the matron came in again and made a big to-do about counting off by two's, breaking up obvious couples. Frances and a thin, nervous-looking girl she hadn't noticed before were led down a hall lit more or less by fifteen-watt bulbs and shown into a cell about nine feet square, with cots along two walls and an uncovered toilet. There didn't seem to be much to say. They sat down and waited. Finally the matron came back with two trays on which were plates of food, spoons and forks, plastic tumblers of water. "You can keep the water glasses."

The food was greasy—fried potatoes, hamburgers, canned

peas, a slice of bread with a square of butter on top. "They have it sent in," Frances's roommate explained. They ate in silence.

The afternoon stretched ahead endlessly. She sat up on the cot, fingering the mattress covered in striped ticking and the folded gray camp blanket. No sheets. Wish I had a book, she thought; never go anywhere without a book after this. Nobody had examined her pocketbook; she dumped its contents out on the cot and looked for something that would help pass the time. After she had filed her nails down to the quick and made up her face, which felt dry and gritty, there was nothing else to do. Her hands felt sticky. There were a small enamel basin and pitcher on a stand in the corner, but no water.

"They'll bring you water tomorrow, before breakfast. Shower twice a week."

"How do you—"

"Been in before."

Suppose I never get out? She thought wildly. It was silly, she knew. But it was all she could do not to rattle the door and scream, like somebody in a B-grade movie.

She thought about the girl with the earring, who now seemed like an old and cherished friend. From down the hall came a sound of hysterical crying, then a burst of hysterical laughter, quickly hushed. The matron came around gathering up trays, dishes, silverware.

Frances said, "I want to make a phone call."

"I'll ask the sergeant."

She had a five and three singles in her billfold, and perhaps a dollar's worth of change in the coin purse. She folded the five small and held it out. A gleam in the policewoman's eyes assured her that she was on the right track. She shoved the money into the woman's hand, looking the other way.

"My friend will take care of everything when she comes."

The matron went away.

She waited.

"Uh, miss. You can call your friend now."

"Thank you."

The phone was down the hall, an old-fashioned wall style

instrument a little too high for her. She stood on tiptoe, and dialed Bake's number with a trembling finger. The ringing went on and on.

"Hello?"

Wonderful relief flooded through her. Her knees shook so that she had to lean against the dingy wall. "This is me."

"Oh."

"Look, I'm in jail. I don't even know where it is." She looked toward the matron, who was frankly listening. The woman gave the address. "They're letting people out on bail, or something. I don't even know how much."

"Probably fifty," Bake said, as though it mattered.

"Will you come over and get me out?"

"Look, baby, I'm sorry as hell about this, I feel like a traitor, running out on you . . . But it wouldn't have done you a damn bit of good if they'd taken me along, now would it? I'd have been charged with assault or something. She was out cold." She stopped. Frances waited, digging her nails into the flesh of her hands. In the background, at Bake's end of the line, someone asked a question. The voice, vaguely suspended in mid-query, sounded familiar. Bake answered distinctly. Then she said, "Look, baby, I haven't got any money. And even if I did I couldn't walk in there. Somebody might identify me."

"What am I supposed to do, stay here the rest of my life?"

Bake said reluctantly, "I don't like this any better than you do, but it looks like you better call Bill."

"Oh, I can't!"

"He'd come down and bail you out, wouldn't he?"

"I guess so, but I couldn't do that."

"Well, what else can you do?"

Bake said, "I'm worried sick about you, baby. Call me the minute you get out, will you?"

Frances hung up without answering.

The matron asked, "When will your friend get here?"

Frances looked at her. Malice overlay her thick features. "As soon as she can." She wanted to cry, but there was no place where she could be alone.

The cell door swung shut behind her.

Supper was soup and meat sandwiches. Her cellmate refused food with a mute shake of her head and lay down on one of the cots, pulling the scratchy blanket up and turning her face to the wall. Frances ate absentmindedly, her mind a turmoil of bewilderment and raw, bleeding hurt.

Why? Why had Bake done this to her? She felt that nothing—not disgrace, not the fear of jail, not even the danger of being identified and tried and imprisoned—could have kept her from Bake, if their roles had been reversed. Besides, it was impossible for her to imagine Bake timid or frightened. Bake, who drove better half-drunk than most people did sober, who walked for miles and disciplined her good sturdy body, who thought things out clearly and spoke her mind without any reservations—this wasn't the girl to take a flight from trouble.

Maybe if I could understand, Frances thought miserably, it wouldn't hurt so.

If I could only figure out why she did it. She must have had a reason.

"You got any water?"

Frances handed over the glass, only half aware of what she was doing. The girl said, "God, I'm thirsty," and took it in trembling hands. She handed back the empty tumbler and lay down again, her face turned away.

The lights in the hall burned all night. Like a hospital, Frances thought, remembering Bob's birth and the time she had her appendix out. The women in the next cell were whispering together; she could hear their voices, but she couldn't make out the words. She wished she had someone to talk to. At last she took off her shoes and lay down, uncomfortable in her clothes but not wanting to undress further in so public a place or to touch the grimy blanket.

She slept finally, too exhausted to stay awake but uncomfortable and conscious of the harsh mattress cover and matted, stale-smelling wool blanket. Her skin itched, her face felt dirty. She wanted a bath.

She had been awake several times, falling back into an

uneasy doze each time, when the sound of crying jolted her wide awake. Her cellmate was walking the floor, moaning, clutching her arms across her front.

Frances said, "What's the matter?" There was no answer, "Are you sick?"

The girl turned a drawn face to her. "My stomach hurts."

A policeman came to the door of the cell. "What's the matter here?"

"She doesn't feel good."

She hardly expected him to do anything about it, but he did: he went away and came back in a few minutes with a stocky young man who, although in shirtsleeves and badly in need of a shave, had a doctor's air of being in command. He turned on the light in the cell, took the moaning girl by the shoulder and turned her around. He pulled down one eyelid, then the other; rolled up her sleeve and looked minutely at her thin upper arm.

"Oh Christ, another one. Come on, honey, we'll give you something to make you feel better."

Frances asked, "What's the matter with her?"

"She needs a fix, that's all. Your girlfriend?"

"No, I never saw her before."

He led the girl away. Frances was alone.

The bathtub at home was white and clean. The linen closet was full of fresh towels and there were new bars of soap wrapped in colored paper. More than anything in the world, she wanted to get into a tubful of hot water and scrub this day's dirt off herself.

In the morning, a sleepy-eyed policeman brought oatmeal and coffee. She wasn't hungry. I'll eat when I get home, she thought. When the matron came back to take the tray, she asked for permission to call her husband.

13

BILL WAS WAITING AT THE DESK. THERE WERE dark smudges above his cheekbones and sharp vertical lines between his eyes. He looked tired, but his suit was pressed and he wore a sober knitted tie. Not the kind of man you expect to find in a police station, bailing out his wayward wife.

She was surprised to see, when they passed a drugstore on the way to the car and she caught a glimpse of her reflection in the plate-glass door, that she didn't look particularly wayward. She felt dirty and messy, her head ached, her arm and leg muscles were tired. But she looked mild and refined, like a schoolteacher of whom it could only be said, damningly, that she still looked young. She got into the car and nervously smoothed her skirt, which was wrinkled from being slept in.

Bill started the car.

The only words she had heard him say were, "Thank you," to the policeman who had escorted her into his presence. She wondered nervously how to break the ice that seemed to be thickening around them. I'm sorry. (The penitent note.) It wasn't my fault. (Too defensive.) This has certainly been an interesting experience. (Flippant.)

She put out a tentative hand. "Bill—"

"Skip it." He didn't sound unkind, merely preoccupied. She pulled back her hand as though he had struck her. They drove in silence for what seemed like a long time. They pulled up in front of the house and sat waiting, making no move to get out. Finally she realized that he was waiting for her to leave. "I have to get to work," he said without changing expression. "I'm late already."

She wondered whether he had gone to the office the day before, but was afraid to ask him. He was a silent stranger.

She scrambled out of the car and watched him drive away, absurdly like a hostess speeding the departing guest.

The house was quiet and rather chilly—of course, Bill would have turned the thermostat down no matter how upset he was. She walked through the downstairs rooms, feeling like an intruder. The furniture was a little dusty, but everything was neat. There were dishes piled in the kitchen sink—no more dishes than she was accustomed to finding there after a day at work. Either Bill and Bob had eaten out, or they had washed their dishes. Or else—and this brought a pang of guilt like a physical pain—they had been too worried to be hungry. She pictured them sitting at opposite ends of the dinette table, heavy eyed from anxiety and lack of sleep, picking at their food.

It wasn't any picnic for me either, she thought resentfully. None of it was my fault. I didn't want to go to Karla's in the first place. That was Bake's doing. And besides, Bill's stayed out all night plenty of times, and how do I know what he does? As least I didn't come home drunk.

At least, a small reproving inner voice reminded her, you've never had to bail him out. She plodded upstairs, and stood looking vaguely at the furnishings of her own bedroom. The covers were folded back neatly from the unmade bed, Bill's chiffonier drawers were closed, the window was open the usual four inches. She closed it, shivering in the cold wind. The trinkets on her dressing table looked unfamiliar. She went into the bathroom and turned on the hot water, feeling the dull throb of headache behind her eyes.

Bill didn't need her. Bake had told her so a hundred times, and she had agreed. In long discussions over the luncheon table, in the dreamy relaxation that followed love, in their increasingly frequent quarrels Bake had insisted that Bill no longer needed her, that she meant nothing to him. It was a statement worn meaningless by repetition, like the Lord's Prayer or the Pledge of Allegiance. Now she realized with sharp terror that Bake had been right all along. Bill really didn't need her. He was at work all day and out on business most evenings, he had his own circle of friends, his interests were foreign to her. He was no longer the man she had married. And she had changed. If she let him, he would no doubt marry again. In a year's time she would be forgotten.

She was in the tub, lathered thick as whipped cream, when the phone rang. It took three rings for her to wrap a towel around herself and run dripping down the stairs, half panicky, half hopeful.

"Hello?"

"Frankie. Baby. Are you all right?"

She shivered. "I'm fine."

"I wondered about you all night. I'm a wreck." Bake sounded

anxious, whether for Frances or herself it was hard to say. "Is anyone with you?"

"No, I'm alone. The men in my family don't seem to care whether I'm alive or dead."

"They'd have been notified if you were dead. What do you want them to do, stand around and bawl because you're back home safe?"

"Well—"

"Look; I have to see you. I've cancelled all my appointments for today anyway. Why don't you come over?"

Remember she ran out on you. "I'm pretty tired." Frances said hesitantly.

"That makes two of us. You can take a nap over here. I'll fix you some hot milk or something."

Frances stood uncertainly holding the telephone. Beyond the living room window she could see the house next door, a stodgy building of tan brick set in a square of dead grass. The rattling stalks of last summer's flowers drooped above a patch of bare earth. It was a dispiriting sight. She said reluctantly, "I really ought to go to the office."

"Call in and tell them you're sick."

"Well, I could do that."

"Baby, I have to see you."

"Okay, I'll come." She would have to take a taxi; it was cold outside and her hair was dripping wet. She would have to telephone the office. She would—oh, to hell with it. Anything was better than spending a day alone in this silent house. She said, "I'll be there in half an hour."

Bake was waiting at the door of the apartment. At the sight of her, all the loneliness and resentment melted out of Frances's heart. She was in Bake's arms, and her head was on Bake's shoulder, and everything was all right.

She said, sobbing, "I don't ever want to go through anything like that again."

"It's pretty horrible," Bake said. "It happened to Jane and me once. That's one reason I didn't want to be picked up again." She disentangled herself to wave at a confusion of newspapers on the studio couch. "It's all right, the fool's going to get well and they didn't give any names."

The Tribune and *Sun Times* had about six lines apiece, on inside pages, stating that police had been called when an unidentified woman struck a second woman, also unidentified, at the Club Karla on the near North Side. The victim has been taken to a nearby hospital for emergency treatment and was recovering at her home from a slight concussion. There was no mention of the mass arrest and no suggestions that Karla's was anything but a run-of-the-mill night spot.

Frances took a deep breath. "What a relief!"

"The other papers didn't even mention it." From the crumpled confusion on the couch, it was plain that Bake had made a thorough search. "Was it pretty bad?"

"It wasn't good." She followed Bake into the kitchen and sat perched on the tall stool, arms around knees.

Bake busied herself with bottles and glasses. "You need a drink."

"That's for sure."

The apartment was pleasantly warm, the little kitchen bright and neat under the overhead light. She remembered the Sunday last spring when they had painted the walls and cupboards, a day that began with a vast epicurean breakfast at noon and ended in a wild all-absorbing bout in bed at two the next morning, dredging them up exhausted and hung over on the arid shores of Monday morning. If I belong anywhere, she thought, it's here. This is home.

Bake handed her a glass, and stood soberly looking down at her. "I hate myself. I've been to hell and back."

"You couldn't help it."

"Darling, why do you let me get so plastered?"

Frances said with a trace of bitterness, "Because I can't do anything with you."

Bake said slowly, "Oh yes, you can. There are a great many things you can do with me."

Frances was silent. A slow warmth generated by alcohol and desire was beginning to grow within her, dispelling the fatigue and loneliness. It spread from the pit of her stomach up into her chest and arms, then down. Wonderful, after being chilled so long.

She held out her glass. "Got anymore?"

"Sure."

They sat in comfortable silence for a while. Bake yawned. She had on pajamas, an old pair she kept for camping trips and the like; her hair was ruffled; she sat with her bare feet propped up on a kitchen chair. Frances had seen her like this a hundred times, and it always filled her with a deep secret happiness. Bake, indolent and relaxed, was so different from her self-possessed public self as to give Frances a feeling of ownership—as though she had a written treasure of whose very existence other people were unaware. She sat looking at Bake, knowing that she was going to want to touch her pretty soon but in no hurry, relishing her leisure.

"Matter, baby?"

"I was just thinking that I don't have to be home till almost six o'clock."

"Doesn't leave you much time. It's twenty past ten now."

Frances refilled her glass. "Don't let me drink too much. It makes me sleepy."

"Do you good to catch a nap. We don't want you falling apart."

The press of desire was becoming urgent. She moved across the kitchen, glass in hand, walking carefully because quite suddenly her legs seemed to belong to somebody else. She laid a hand on Bake's shoulder. "Darling."

"Yes."

In the two years of their relationship she had approached Bake perhaps a dozen times. It was Bake, aggressive and experienced, who initiated their lovemaking, suggested experiments, set the time and place. Frances had been content to have it that way. Now she stood wordless, afraid of being rebuffed, feeling the slow imperative rise of her love and unable to ask for what she wanted. She looked questioningly down into Bake's face.

Bake stoop up. "Come on, baby. Come to bed."

14

AWAKE, BABY?"

Frances stirred. "Mmm."

"It's four o'clock. You've been asleep for hours. I took a little nap myself," Bake said, smiling.

"That's nice," Frances said. She opened her eyes, trying to bring the room into focus. "Was I—all right?"

"You were wonderful."

"Know something?"

"What's that?"

"I love you."

Bake laughed softly. "Big surprise."

Frances rolled over. "Ooh, you're nice and warm. I wish I didn't have to get up.

"You never want to get up, you lazy bum." Bake's arms were warm and gentle around her, no hunger in them now. "I don't like to have to get up, either."

Frances sat up, pulling the blanket closer around her shoulders. "Got a cigarette?"

"Here." Bake lit two cigarettes, took a puff of each, and handed her one; the small ritual after love that was part of their closeness. Frances smiled, taking it. "Ashtray?"

"I moved the stand around to your side," Bake stopped abruptly, as though someone had put a hand over her mouth.

Frances smiled, seeing in her mind's eye Bake starving off anxiety by shoving the furniture around. It was so at variance with all the things that made up the daytime Bake—and so in keeping with her private gentleness and concern. She reached for the glass ashtray.

Her smile froze.

There were four butts in the ashtray, two stained with the dark-red lipstick Bake used, two with a soft mauve pink.

"What's the matter?"

"Have you changed your lipstick?"

"Oh." Bake's face closed, as Frances had seen it do when people probe too close for comfort. A courteous evasion would be forthcoming—or an expedient lie. "Jane was here a while yesterday. She took a nap."

For a moment she almost believed it. She wanted to believe it. It was such a reasonable, comforting explanation, and the truth opened on such a wild vista of desolation. Then she looked again at the four stained and twisted cigarette ends. Two each, smoked in the leisurely relaxation of after-love; this was their pattern, hers and Bake's. Now she knew where Bake had learned it, how it came to be habitual with her.

Frances said in a strangled whisper, "Jane was here—with you. You made love with her the way you do with me."

"Frances, look, I've never lied to you. I'm no good at lies." Bake caught her by the shoulder, turned her until their eyes met. "I've know Jane for years, ever since I first came to Chicago. We're old friends."

"That's a good name for it."

"I suppose you've never slept with anybody else, like your husband, for instance."

"I wouldn't mind so much if it were somebody else."

"That's a lot of crap. You'd mind no matter who I slept with—and I guess I would too if it were the other way around."

Bake shook her head as though to clear the sleep out of it. "Look, would you feel better if I said it didn't mean anything to either of us? It was just something that happened."

"Those things don't just happen."

"Sure they do. You're with someone you like, you have a few drinks, and wham! There you are. It doesn't mean a thing."

"I suppose she's better at it than I am. I don't know anything except what I've learned from you."

Bake grinned. "Complaining?"

"No." Frances started to cry; she couldn't help it. Bake sat quietly looking at her for a while. "Look, baby, you're over tired. You wouldn't feel so bad about this if you weren't so tired. You've had a bad couple of days."

"That hasn't got anything to do with it."

"All right, goddamn it, I went to bed with Jane, I called her up, if you want to know. What was I supposed to do, sit here chewing my nails, wondering what was happening to you and whether that woman was going to be all right or not? All I wanted was somebody to talk to. Neither of us planned the rest of it. You have to believe that."

"Then why did you do it?"

"Oh God, Frankie, these things happen. Jane probably feels just as bad as you do. She and Kay had been together almost four years—ever since—well, anyway, can't you just drop the whole thing?"

That sounded reasonable. The trouble was, there was no reason in the way she felt. She was hurt, yes, and jealous. With the familiar cycle of fatigue, desire, passion, and relaxation, her weariness had cleared away and she was able to react emotionally again.

She rocked back and forth on the bed, in actual pain.

"I don't think I can stand this."

"Will you listen to me, or do I have to knock some sense into you? I went with Jane for a while when I first came to town, sure. She wasn't the first one, either. You didn't think I never cared for anybody else, did you?"

"I don't care how many other—"

"As if going to bed was all there is to it." Bake's voice was scornful. "There's liking each other, being friends. Reading the same books and listening to the same music. Thinking the same things are funny." She took a deep breath. "There's caring. I care what happens to you."

"I found that out yesterday." As though triggered by her own scorn, Frances got out of bed and began pulling on her clothes. One stocking ripped from hem to toe, but she gartered it tightly and put on her shoes. "I'm going home now."

"Look, let's not fight."

"I'm not fighting." She turned wide, hurt eyes on Bake. "Maybe I'll get over this some time."

Bake swung her feet over the edge of the bed, slid her arms into a terry housecoat. "I'm sorry. Maybe it would have been better if I'd lied to you."

"It wouldn't have done any good. I always had a funny feeling about Jane. Now I know why. I always knew," Frances said slowly, in wonder, "but I wouldn't let myself know."

"I'm sorry."

They walked to the door together, not touching. Bake held it open impassively. "Remember, this is your idea, not mine. I'll be around when you get to feeling better."

Frances didn't answer. All the way down the endless stairs she was conscious of Bake standing there, watching her go.

Now what? She asked herself, slumped into the corner of the taxi. She couldn't go back to Bake; she never wanted to see Bake again. She couldn't go home, to Bill's house. She thought wildly of a hotel, and then realized that she had less than two dollars in her purse, not even enough for a cheap room. Besides, that would be a temporary solution. What she had to find was an answer.

The streets were crowded with salespeople and office works getting out for the day. She stopped the cab at the corner of State and Lake, gave the driver all the money she had except fifty cents, and wandered aimlessly for several blocks. There was a kind of comfort, or at least distraction, in lights and crowds; the excitement of color and motion. She stopped several times to look in store windows, without really seeing the merchandise on display.

She was getting chilled. The wind was ominous of snow, and her coat was thin. She went into a drugstore and ordered coffee. It was Thursday night, late closing for Loop department stores, and the fountain was crowded with shoppers and store person-nel. Housewives, high-school kids drinking cokes and eating hamburgers, tired salesgirls, grabbing a quick cheap meal. She drank the coffee black and hot, thankful for the warmth and stimulus of it, unwilling to get up and leave the brightness of the store.

"You alone?"

She looked up, startled. The woman was somewhere between fifty and sixty, thin to emaciation, with rolling, veined eyes and a long corded neck. "Don't you remember me? I saw you at Karla's one night. You were with a dark-haired girl. She's not with you tonight, though."

"No," Frances said. She put a nickel under the edge of the saucer and stood up, clutching her check and a dime.

The woman stepped into her way. "You look sort of beat. Is there anything I can do for you, dear? Anything at all?" She looked hopeful. "Would you like a drink? Maybe you'd like to come home with me for a drink?"

"No thanks." Oh God, Frances thought in pure terror, is that what I'm becoming? Is that me in twenty years? She said coldly, "I think you've made a mistake. I have an appointment with my husband."

"Oh, now look—"

"I'm in a hurry."

She pushed her way to the cashier and paid for her coffee, ignoring the stares of the other customers.

It was beginning to snow. The sidewalks were slippery with half-frozen slush, and a cold wind blew off Lake Michigan. Frances shivered. The soles of her shoes would be soaked through in a few minutes, and she was already chilled to the bone.

Where do you go when there's no place you belong?

She sneezed. It's no time to be melodramatic, she admonished herself. Go home, get into a hot tub, take a couple of aspirins and get into bed.

She got into a southbound bus and sat huddled miserably next to a fat salesman with a smelly cigar, trying to think about the mess she had made of her life, but only able to think of her warm, waiting bed.

15

WE GOING TO HAVE A CHRISTMAS TREE THIS year?" Frances studied her son's face. It was a replica of Bill's only a little younger now than the face Bill had worn when she first knew him. He was as tall as Bill and as broad, too, and his hands were those of a grown man, hard from tennis and basketball and the summer job, with hair on the backs. A boy's question in a man's voice, making her smile.

"Of course, Christmas tree and all the fixings. Why?"

"Nothing." He leaned against the door jamb, watching her as she moved from sink to table to stove.

She slid a panful of cookies into the oven and closed the door carefully. "What's on your mind?"

"Nothing." But he didn't meet her eyes. "You suppose you could call Mari up and invite her for Christmas dinner?"

"Why, I guess so."

In spite of his casual tone, she knew suddenly that this meant a lot to him. He had been thinking about it for a while, trying to think of an approach that was sufficiently casual, because it meant so much.

"She's a nice girl. Only won't her family want her at home on Christmas Day?"

"Aw, they eat at night. I'm going over then."

"Think you can eat two holiday meals?"

Bob grinned. "I'll pass up the bread and potatoes," he said, sounding eighteen again. "You called her up and invited her, huh?"

"Why so formal all of a sudden? You've been bringing kids home for meals as long as I can remember."

He said gravely, "Mari is no kid."

She looked at him sharply, disquieted as she had been by her first glimpse of the girl's serene, close face. He reddened. She was aware of a mixture of emotions: amusement at the sight of her boy putting on man's ways, tenderness for the child he had been, nostalgia for the days when the three of them had really been a family, resentment because his growing up meant that her own youth was slipping away.

She said flatly, "Sure, I'll call her up if it means so much to you."

"Thanks."

She bent to turn the oven down a trifle, and straightened up to tear yesterday's page off the wall calendar. December twenty-four. Five years ago she would have been downtown, on the day before Christmas, jostled by tired shoppers, trying to spread the saved-up grocery money over all the things Bob wanted. Toys were marked down on the day before Christmas, and so were trees in the open-air lots.

She said aloud, "Remember the little table tree we had in Fayetteville?" and turned to catch Bob's answer, but he was gone. Off to tell his girl she was going to be officially invited to dinner, she supposed.

You wouldn't catch Bill Ollenfield lugging home a bargain tree on Christmas Eve this year, getting spruce needles all over his old jacket, staying up until after midnight to hang the colored lights and dime-store trinkets and the silver tinsel. He would be at the office, going over his damned old reports and adding up the take from the pre-Christmas boom. Plastic Playthings were on every dime-store counter in the United States, she guessed. Cheap junk, most of them would be broken by New Year's Day, but they were important enough to keep a busy executive from his family. If he stayed home all day on the twenty-fifth she would be surprised.

She supposed he had a present for her, something or other his secretary had picked up on her lunch hour, gift wrapped by Carson's or Marshall Field's professional wrapping service. He didn't have to go without lunches anymore in order to buy her a pair of nylons or a small bottle of perfume. She had bought him a watch, ten dollars down and ten a month until it was paid for, hoping against hope that the generosity of the gift would crack the polite impersonality that had formed around him, like a thin coating of ice. As a gift it didn't really mean anything.

There would have to be a gift for Mari too, something impersonal but good—not an easy decision to make. She suspected that Mari was selective about her possessions, was used to having the best.

Well, she couldn't call Mari until Bob got back. She didn't know the girl's phone number or address. She tried to put out of her mind the memory of Bob's young face so intent and full of love, of Mari's pure oval at once serene and so unrevealing. This was more than another girl friend. I feel like a mother-in-law, she thought, wryly.

The front door opened and shut again. Bill came through the

house, shedding his overcoat on the davenport as he passed, dropping his briefcase on the coffee table. He stood in the doorway as Bob had done, taking in the fragrance of browning dough and the clutter of baking utensils on the dinette table.

Frances said, "Hi," looking away from him, her hands busy. He didn't answer.

Stubborn as a mule, she thought. She ran hot water into a mixing bowl.

He took down a whiskey bottle from the top shelf of the cupboard, poured a little into a plastic tumbler, and stood sipping it slowly, looking away from her.

There was a smell of scorching, a puff of acrid smoke. She rushed to the oven and pulled out the cookie sheet. At the sight of the charred lumps she began to cry, idiotically. Bill set down his glass.

"Scrape it in the garbage," he said a little thickly. "It's no great loss."

Anger flamed in her. "Thanks. If that's all you've got to say, you might as well keep still."

"You haven't got anything to complain of." Bill refilled the glass, his hand shaking so that a little of the clear liquid spilled over. "You've got it pretty soft."

"Have I? You haven't said a decent word to me since—"

"Go ahead and say it. Since you and your crummy friends went to jail." His face darkened. "I suppose that was my fault."

"Yes, it was—if you really want to know. You don't even know I'm alive. You're so wrapped up in your damned old plastics business you don't have any room in your life for human beings." She was good and angry now, all the accumulated resentment of the last few years coming to a rolling boil. "You don't need me. You wouldn't even care if I got out of here and let you marry somebody else—you'd probably be glad. You aren't human."

"What I can't see is, what are you complaining about? Because I bailed you out, or because I don't make love to you as often as you might like, or what?"

"Well, you haven't been very friendly."

"Okay." Bill's face was flushed. He had put on weight in the last few months; his belly was beginning to round out under the white shirt, and he had the first sag of a double chin. His eyes were bloodshot, whether from overwork or alcohol, she couldn't tell. He had begun drinking, probably before he came home. His own office was officially closed for the day but salesmen would have been in from out of town, and he might have made the rounds of other people's office parties before drifting in.

"Okay," he said again. "Come upstairs, if you're so damn anxious to be noticed."

"Don't be silly."

"Come on."

She took a silver knife from the drawer and began to scratch at the burned baking sheet.

He seized her wrist. The knife clattered to the floor. "By God, I've taken a lot from you, but I'm not going to take any more. Come on upstairs, or I'll drag you up."

His hand was like steel. She tried to pull away. His grip tightened. "Upstairs," he said and the quietness of his voice was a threat.

She followed him up the back stairs step by step, balking at each one, pulled along by the implacable band of fingers around her wrist.

He shut the bedroom door behind them before he let her go. Then he pulled down the shade, making dusk in the room, shutting out the cold winter light and the suddenly friendly, everyday view of street and houses. Frances stood warily by the wall, seeing the room where she had slept so many nights suddenly become an alien and a frightening place, a prison.

She said coldly, "You're drunk."

"Not too drunk for what I'm going to do. You don't need to worry about that." He caught her by the shoulder as she edged toward the door. "Anyhow," he said, "you seem to like your friends that way."

He stripped off her clothes like a farmer husking corn, and threw her down on the bed so hard the springs rattled. She shut her eyes.

He was quick and violent, a stranger seeking fast relief, using her for his own need and unaware of her as a person. Like a man in a two-dollar whorehouse, she thought, despising the woman and in a hurry to get away. In almost no time he was done with her. He rolled over and sat on the edge of the bed, white in the cold half-light. A faint stale odor of alcohol hung around him.

She lay without moving or speaking, too miserable even to pull up the covers.

He got into his clothing quickly and efficiently, as though he were getting up to go to work. At the door he turned, looking uncertain for the first time. "Frances—"

She didn't answer.

She lay there for a long time after the downstairs door slammed. At last she began to shiver in the cold air. She drew the sheet up around her chin. Immediately, as though the motion had set her thoughts to wheeling, reality pressed in upon her. She lay looking at nothing, reliving the events of the last few hours. The pleasure of working in her clean, light kitchen, a pleasure she had almost forgotten since she started going to business, intensified by the making of holiday cookies. I was almost happy, she thought in wonder. It seemed to her that she hadn't been happy for a long time.

The odd mixture of feelings that rippled the surface of her mind when Bob spoke of the girl, Mari. Quick admiration for one so young and in every way desirable, followed by the jealously of a maturing woman for a young one and then by the fear of losing Bob to an early marriage. And the quick blazing up of her anger at Bill, held in check so long, like a fire that has smoldered for a long time and then, fanned by a sudden wind, shoots up to the sky. It had made her feel good to be angry, like having a clean sharp pain after months of a dull nagging infection.

Then, suddenly, the indignity of being dragged upstairs bodily by a man half drunk for the discharge of a passion that was more hate than love. She felt violated. She felt dirty, as though she would never be clean again. She lay with her hands outside the covers, as though her skin were unclean to the touch.

But this was nothing new. She had been through this before—

the cringing sickness, the dull wish that she could shut her eyes on the whole confused mess and never open them again, the dragging fatigue. She lay slack muscled, her hands lax against the bedspread, remembering.

16

SHE HAD BEEN TOO TIRED, THE SECOND NIGHT after her mother's death, to be capable of emotion. The sights and smells of a cancer patient's dying were incredible. She didn't blame her father for staying away and, when he did come home, taking the edge off his misery with a drink. She came back from the graveyard to a house put in unaccustomed order by the neighborhood women, a kitchen table loaded with offerings of food: ham, potato salad, cake, pie. After the weeks of unremitting work, there was suddenly nothing to do.

The afternoon was endless. She thought about writing to Miss Putnam—Miss Putnam had sent flowers and a note. But there was nothing to say. She was staying in this place she hated, taking over the drudgery, because there was nothing else to do. She accepted it. But the hurt was still too new and raw to admit of words. She sat on the living room cot, her hands—callused, water soaked, stubby nailed—idle in her lap.

I can't go through with it.

You have to.

She must have dozed, for some time later she woke, startled frightened. For a moment she thought she was back in the dorm, awake by the clangor of Sondy's alarm clock. Then realization flooded in. She got up stiffly and walked to the window, aching in every muscle. The children were playing in the dusk, still in their new clothes. She called them in, gave them ham, cake, potato salad. She made coffee and sat at the kitchen table drinking it, too weary to swallow solid food.

Lorena said, "Pa went off someplace. I hate Pa."

"Never mind that. Wipe the crumbs off your face, then pick

up these dishes for me—that's a good girl." Frankie smiled thinly. "I'll take care of Pa."

After the children were in bed and the dishes washed, she sat down again on the cot and tried to plan for tomorrow. Pa wouldn't go to work, of course. He was in the tavern at this very minute, not paying for his own drinks tonight but being treated to round after round by his friends and neighbors. At least he's not taking the food out of the children's mouths, she thought. She lit the kerosene lamp and lay down, fixing her gaze on the nimbus of soft yellow light that hovered around the thin glass chimney.

She dozed again. This time she was waked by blundering footsteps across the kitchen floor and the crashing of an overturned chair, followed by a muffled curse. Dead drunk, of course. It was what she had expected. She got to her feet.

Joe Kirby swayed in the doorless space between the living room and bedroom, clutching at the jamb for steadiness. The smell of whiskey preceded him into the room, and his eyes were bloodshot. Oh, sure, Frankie thought, he wouldn't be drinking beer tonight. Bottled in bond, that's what it would be, paid for out of someone else's grocery money. There would be some husbands getting hell tomorrow.

He wavered in her direction. "Nancy, honey."

She had never seen him this far gone. Muddled, yes, and bad tempered beyond reason, but not out of his head. He thinks I'm Ma, she realized. Slipped a cog somewhere. She said coldly, "Why don't you go to bed and sleep it off?"

"Nancy, you look so pretty."

She moved away, warily. The old childish fear of him held her spellbound for a moment. Then their new cold determination took over. "You're disgusting. Go to bed."

"Come on with me, then." He stood in front of her, wavering.

"Come on, honey. You and me's gonna have a real good time together."

She was seized by sudden teeth-chattering panic.

He reached for her, missed, and moved in closer. Her back

was to the old cot where she had slept since babyhood. The wall was behind her, the door on the opposite side of the room. There was a window at the foot of the cot, screened with cotton mosquito netting. She could squeeze through it if she had to.

But now he had grabbed her and tipped back her head, his breath hot and stinking on her cheek, and she couldn't move.

"Don't be like this, Nancy, honey."

"I'm Frances. You hear me, Frances!" Her voice rose to a shriek. Never mind if the child woke. Anything was better than what she read on his face—naked lust, determined male hunger.

He pushed her back against the cot. The metal frame caught her behind the knees and she went down sprawling.

He'll kill me if I fight back, she thought wildly. An hour before she had been telling herself that she had nothing left to live for. Now all she could think was that she didn't want to die. She was filled with a wild primitive need to survive.

She lay still for a moment, trying to look into his face, trying to focus her eyes on the opposite wall. His grip slacked a little. He shifted position, peering stupidly into her face.

Now.

She brought her right knee up sharply. He howled. She pushed at him. Caught off balance by pain and surprise, he toppled to the floor and sat rocking back and forth, moaning loudly.

She went out of the house, walking past him neither slowly nor fast, and not looking at him. Outside, a cold early winter wind blew sharply against her sweaty body. She shuddered. But she stayed out huddled against the side of the house for shelter, until she saw through the bedroom window that he had dragged himself to bed and fallen into a sodden sleep.

17 I CAN'T BEAR IT, SHE THOUGHT, TURNING HER head from side to side as Ma had done when the pain got too bad. Men. Dirty, selfish, disgusting— violaters and savages. I'll never let a man touch me again, she thought.

Bill as bad as the rest of them, just like the rest.

This was something she had heard before—she tried, frowning, to remember when and where. Kay, of course, sitting relaxed and easy on Bake's studio couch, one slender leg tucked under her, a cup of coffee in her hand, her dark red hair catching the light.

"Every time he made love to me it was like a declaration of war. It was like being beaten, only worse." She had smiled, and Frances's heart had swelled with understanding and pity. "You'll never get any consideration from a man, anyway. There's no tenderness in them. All they think about is their own satisfaction."

Frances turned restlessly, remembering.

"It takes a woman to understand another woman," Kay said, turning her coffee cup on its saucer and not looking at any of them. "She thinks about the other person, not always about herself. If you're tired, a woman will be gentle and patient—if she loves you. If you're ill she takes care of you. When you're in the mood to make love she knows how to make you feel wonderful. It's better than anything with a man."

And Bake had answered—Frances couldn't remember what, but she could hear Bake's voice hanging soft in the air of the room, agreeing: and she could remember sharply every detail of that night, after the others went home and the logs in the fireplace had burned down to ashes.

Now, she thought, I like Kay. She's wise, she understands things, I wish I could talk to her about Bake. Can't of course, because there's Jane—the whole miserable mess revolves around Jane. She lay thinking about Jane and Kay and the probable implications of their friendship, distracted briefly from her own unhappiness. Kay's too good for her, she thought, picturing Kay's intelligent face with its high cheeckbones, her sensitive mouth, her silky red-brown hair.

A double need began to grow in her. First came the need to be cherished and comforted, a yearning that nobody ever outgrows. She wanted to see Bake and confide everything that had happened, and lay her head on Bake's shoulder and cry a little. She wanted to feel Bake's hands on her body in gentleness, and Bake's cheek laid softly against hers in their own special caress.

That would be enough for a while, she thought, defending herself against any suspicion of lust, since lust had so lately been her undoing.

But under this loneliness that she could acknowledge a stronger hunger began to grow, insistent and clamoring. She began to count the days since she had seen Bake. Almost a month, after two years of being together.

Bill's abrupt and brutal lovemaking, shocking as it had been, had stirred needs in her that were deeper than principle or conscious thought. She turned, throwing the blankets to the floor. Clear in her mind was the picture of Bake standing at the head of the stairs, wrapped snugly in her housecoat, watching an angry unforgiving Frances walk out. How could I do it? She asked herself. How could I be so wicked?

Bake, ivory pale in the moonlight; Bake, tousle headed over morning coffee; Bake, warm and drowsy at three o'clock of a rainy summer daybreak, when lightning crashed across the sky and water streamed down the window.

Bake.

Frances got stiffly out of bed, noting that her knees ached when she stood up and that an ugly purple bruise was forming inside her right thigh. Her clothes lay in an untidy pile where Bill had thrown them, one shoe upside down on her wool skirt, her stockings curled like empty snake skins. She stepped around them, and pulled her terry robe down from a closet hook.

The telephone waited for her, ready to come to life at her touch. Her finger slipped easily into the dial holes. She waited, scarcely breathing, until the ringing stopped and Bake's voice answered, impersonal and low.

"It's twelve o'clock, baby. Merry Christmas."

"Merry Christmas to you, too." Frances shifted her position so that she could see the bedside clock. "I have to go home."

"Oh God, do we have to go through all that again?"

"I'm sorry. Bob's girl is coming for dinner, and some people later."

She could see the Flanagan's faces if they arrived and found her missing. She started to giggle, then stopped, warned by the tight look around Bake's mouth. "I know it sounds silly. I hate it being this way, but I have to go. I can't get out of it."

"It's up to you. If you'd rather spend the day being a nice little hausfrau—"

"I don't want to. I don't want to go home at all."

"Don't let me stop you."

"Darling do we have to be like this?"

"Well, you can't expect me to be happy about the way you're carrying on." Bake got to her feet and stretched, yawning. "First you're all set to leave your husband and move in here—I was running around trying to find a lawyer for you, I suppose you meant it when you were through with Bill. The next thing I know you're flouncing out of the place in a tantrum. Never going to speak to me again. I know, I know," she said, motioning for Frances not to interrupt, "you were mad at me. We don't have to go through that all over again, do we? So now you come back and everything's going to be fine. Except you still think more of that damn man than you do of me."

"I don't. I wish I never had to see him again."

"He's worse than stodgy and stupid, he's vicious too. Look at the bruises on you. Well," Bake said, "there's a masochist for every sadist, but I didn't have you pegged for one."

"Look, I'd just as soon leave him. I'm going to leave him. Only I can't walk out on Christmas Day."

"Why not?"

"Oh Bake, don't spoil everything."

Bake sat down on the edge of the bed, reaching for a cigarette. Frances's eyes filled with tears. I don't want to fight, she thought. We never used to fight. Now we're getting edgy with each other, like a husband and wife who have outgrown affection but are still bound together by habit and physical need. It's all wrong.

She turned her face away, wiping her wet eyes on the hem of the pillowcase. In childish needs of reassurance, she grasped at the little ritual that had ended so many hours together.

"Bake, give me a cigarette."

Bake handed her the package.

"Oh, never mind. I have to hurry."

"Now what's the matter?"

"Nothing."

Realization crossed Bake's face. She took another cigarette, scratched one of her kitchen matches across the underside of the night stand. "You're being pretty infantile."

Hurt swelled Frances's throat so she couldn't answer. She got up quickly, gathered her clothes from the slipper chair and carried them into the bathroom. Bake sat watching her, narrow eyed. Then she stubbed out her own cigarette and followed.

"Look, baby, you're making something out of nothing."

Frances reached for her blue toothbrush, hanging companionably beside Bake's red one. Over a mouthful of foam she turned hurt and anxious eyes on Bake.

"You're so damn possessive." Bake sat down gingerly on the edge of the tub. "Ouch, this is cold. Look, you can't own the people you care for. If love isn't a free gift, then it's nothing."

"Words."

"Okay, I'll give it to you straight. I have a life of my own to live. I can't sit around mooning about you all the time. You don't have to get your feelings hurt every time you turn around."

"My feelings are not hurt."

"They are too. You're madder than hell because I forgot to light your cigarette for you."

Frances said in a low voice. "It's only because you mean so much to me."

"Nobody'd ever guess it. Look, you can stay here if you want to. We have all day, a whole day with nobody else barging in. But no, you'd rather go back to that place and knock yourself out cooking a big dinner for that creep you're married to. After he as good as raped you."

"I'm not doing it for him. Can't you get that through your head?"

"Go ahead, go. Maybe he'll give you another good going over tonight. Won't that be fun?"

"Oh, shut up!" It was the first time she had ever yelled at

Bake and they were both astounded. Frances blinked back the hot tears. "I'm sorry."

"I'm sorry too. Only it might be a good idea to make up your mind whether you're my girl or Bill's wife, don't you think? These double-gaited people who keep switching back and forth make me kind of sick to my stomach."

Frances began to pull on her clothes. There was nothing else she could say. Technically, she supposed Bake was right, and had cause to be aggrieved. Certainly she had been going to bed with Bill whenever he seemed to expect it, which hadn't been very often, because there was no reasonable excuse she could make for refusing his attentions. She was married to him, wasn't she? She had even found some pleasure in his lovemaking at times, although she tried to be passive in his arms—a whore's trick, she thought in quick self-contempt.

After all, it was Bake's fault. Bake's caress had stirred and wakened her, taught her what passion could be. She had even thought, furtively and guiltily, how wonderful it would be if Bill would do what Bake did, and then . . . Now, remembering this afternoon, she hated herself and him.

"Never again," she said aloud.

"Never again what?"

"I'll never go to bed with him again."

"I've heard that before."

"No, I mean it."

"Then you're not even an honest whore. You're nothing but an unpaid housekeeper."

"Maybe I am."

Dressed, she went back into the bedroom, got her coat down off a hanger and put it on. The simple act seemed to push her back into the every day world where her love for Bake was a guilty and exciting secret.

She asked suddenly, "What will you do all day?"

"Go out with some of the girls, probably."

And get a nice edge on, probably, Frances thought, but she managed not to say it. She leaned forward to fix her mouth, squinting a little because the light about the mirror was dim.

"Oh, how pretty."

Bake asked sharply, "What?"

"The locket, here on the dresser." She picked it up, delighted with the design. "Is it new?"

"More or less."

She opened it carefully. The snapshot inside was small but clear. The color drained from her face. "Oh."

Bake turned her face away.

"You've been seeing Jane?"

"Of course I have. We're old friends."

"She gave you this, didn't she?"

"Any reason she shouldn't?"

No reason, Frances thought quickly. Except that I didn't give you a Christmas present this year, or you me. Except that I was sitting home with a broken heart. Except that a gold locket with a picture in it isn't the gift of any casual acquaintance. She laid the bit of jewelry down carefully, as though it might shatter.

"It's not my kind of thing," Bake said. She put her arms around Frances, heavy coat and all. "Other people don't make any difference to us, you know that."

"I know."

But she felt chilled and a little frightened as she tiptoed down the stairs and let herself out into the pitch of the December midnight.

18

FRANCES GOT UP FROM THE UNMADE DAVENport at six o'clock, after four hours of tossing and rolling and trying to find a path through the tangle of problems that was her immediate future. Darkness still pressed against the widows, and the house next door was a black hulk. She stood leaning against the wall, knowing that last night's dishes waited to be washed, but held immobile in a fatigue almost too heavy to bear. If you're going to be a hausfrau, she told herself crossly, you might as well be a good one: God knows you're no good at anything else.

She was having her third cup of coffee, standing, because

to sit down would have been to invite sleep, when Bill came downstairs. For a moment she was too surprised to remember her grievance. "For heaven's sake, it isn't even seven o'clock. Don't tell me you have to go to the office on Christmas."

He blinked drowsily, without answering. She filled another cup and politely handed it to him. He took it and sat down on the step stool. "You didn't come to bed," he said hoarsely.

"I slept down here."

"That wasn't necessary."

"Wasn't it?"

He looked at her with hurt eyes. "I'm sorry about yesterday. That was a stinking thing to do."

"It doesn't matter."

"Try and look at it from my angle for once, will you? Living with you hasn't been any bed of roses lately."

"I said it doesn't matter." She was pleased with herself, her voice was so cold and even. She turned her back on him and began running water into the sink.

He sat looking at her, not knowing what to say. She ignored him. After a few minutes he got up and went into the living room, carrying his cup. She heard him stacking newspapers; then the nasal whine of the vacuum cleaner began. Let him help, she thought. Let him be a Boy Scout and do a good deed every day. It won't get him anywhere.

There was a harsh solace in physical work. As after her mother's death, she found a grim satisfaction and a numbing of mental stress in the aching back and the feeling of urgency that carried her along. By eleven the whole house was in order for guests, even to the hanging of small silly towels in the bathroom. Pies were cooling on the dinette table and the smell of roasting turkey filled the house. Hausfrau, she thought scornfully, wishing in the same breath that she had a real dining room; this eating on card tables was all right for ordinary days, but it would be fun on holidays to have a long dining table and put a white damask cloth on it. The girl from Frisbie, trying to get up in the world.

She went upstairs to change her dress and run a comb

through her hair, noting as she lifted her arm that there was a small bruise just above the elbow. Lust or devotion? She didn't know; there was no way to tell. Probably bumped into something, she told herself sensibly.

Her reflection looked back from the dressing-table mirror, a slender woman with soft brown hair and gray eyes, the brows narrow and winged. She was thinner than she had been two years before, and better groomed; harder, more polished, her mouth a tighter line. Not the sort you suspect of leading a double life. She threw down her pearly button earrings and picked up the copper hoops Bake had given her, but they dangled incongruously against the white collar of her plain wool dress.

She tried not to think about Bake. Don't wonder who's with her. Or what they're doing.

She still had not spoken to Bill when Bob and Mari came in, Bob excited and breathless, Mari calm and pretty. "We went for a walk to get an appetite," Bob said, taking Mari's coat with an air of ownership.

"As if he needed any more appetite," Mari said. "It was nice of you to ask me, Mrs. Ollenfield."

"It was nice of you to come."

The sight of this girl twisted a knife in her heart. Mari was so pretty, so—so exactly right. At the sight of her, the years of wifehood and motherhood rolled away from Frances, and she became again little Frankie Kirby in the outgrown cotton dress, with the skinny arms and legs. This was the kind of girl who had looked at her in the corridors of County High, not meanly but like a citizen of another world who could have nothing in common with such a tacky and squalid creature. This was the kind of girl she would have chosen to be, had she been given the choice.

She said curtly, "Put her coat on a hanger, Bob."

She had to admit that Bill was a good host, probably because of the same qualities that made him a good sales manager. He was affable, he got everyone seated around the card tables (two of them for four diners, because there was so much food), and he watched the plates to be sure everyone was getting enough to eat. With Bob's girl he was at once teasing and flattering, a middle-aged man talking to an attractive teenager, and she was demure with him.

When the Flanagans showed up early, having been invited in for the afternoon, he seemed honestly pleased. "Sooner the better. How about a piece of pie?"

It can't be easy, Frances thought, moved to reluctant admiration. It can't be easy to keep up that kind of front when you're tired or worried—or when your wife is bitchy. She looked at him with unwilling sympathy. Then she recollected that she, not he, was the aggrieved one, and resumed her impassive expression before filling his cup.

Only Betty Flanagan's sharp look made her ask him politely, "More pie?"

He said, "Don't mind if I do. I hate to brag, Jack, but my wife makes the best pie you ever ate."

"In that case, I'll have a big piece."

She had to admit that Bill was showing up well, considering what he had been through in the last few hours. Whatever he might lack, it wasn't courage.

And what about me?

An early dusk was setting in before she could stack the dishes and carry them to the kitchen. Bill made drinks, pulled the shades, turned on the television. I wish I had a drink, Frances thought. A real drink, enough to relax me. Since she had started out with the Flanagans as a total abstainer, she didn't want to invite comments from them now. She thought longingly of the bottle in the top of the cupboard. Maybe a quick one while I'm doing the dishes.

She refused help with the washing up. "I'll stack them." But when she had gotten out the canasta cards and made fresh coffee, Mari followed her into the kitchen. "I'm going to help," she said in her small, composed voice.

"Oh, you don't have to help."

"I will, though."

Frances looked at her. The girl had hardly spoken since her

arrival. She had sat listening to Bob and Bill, laughing at their jokes, eating daintily but with a good appetite.

Frances said, "I'm so glad you could come."

"It was awfully kind of you to ask me."

"Oh, Bob's always having girls here." That'll fix her.

Mari smiled. "I'm always taking boys home, too. But this is different."

Frances turned her face away. "How different?" she asked when she could trust her voice.

"Bob thinks he's in love with me."

"Is he?"

"Maybe." Mari hung a cup on its hook. The unspoken question hung in the air between them. After a moment of silence she answered it. "I'm not sure about it myself, though. I don't want to hurry things. Marriage is too permanent."

"Not always."

"It will be for me. Not because of my religion or anything. But my parents would be miserable if I ever got a divorce. My father's a judge, you know—he's very conservative. But that's not why." Mari hesitated, looking uncertain for the first time in Frances's short knowledge of her. "I want everything to be perfect."

This was a girl who wouldn't do anything on impulse. She would select a husband carefully, taking into account family backgrounds and religion and her husband's career. They taught all this in school now, Frances knew. Mari's children would be carefully spaced and well brought up, her house spotless; she would be president of the PTA and chairman of the women's culture club. She might hold a job before her babies are born or after they begin to grow up, an interesting and well-paid one. A pang for her own hungry, fumbling early years struck Frances's heart, and a regret for the child Bob had been and would never be again.

She said carefully. "You're probably right."

She was conscious again of the small purple bruise above her elbow, and for the second time she wondered whether it had been inflicted by the husband she had come to hate and was beginning to feel sorry for, or by the woman she loved and was beginning to distrust.

She averted her eyes from Mari, feeling guilty.

Mari would never have such a problem. Things would be clear and definite for her. Frances liked her, envied her, and wondered once again: suppose I'd been like that, had that sort of start in life, would things have turned out differently?

The phone rang around eight, while she was making cold turkey sandwiches and thinking, don't these people ever do anything but eat? Bob took it. "For you, Mom." He laid the instrument down and stepped aside, looking at her warily, and, she thought, pleadingly.

It was Bake, more than a little under the influence. "Just wanted to say, Merry Christmas, baby. Jane says it too. Don't you, honey?" There was a small scuffle in the background, then Bake came through again. "You're a sweet kid, Frankie. Too damn serious, though." She had a little trouble with "serious." It came out mangled and she hung up, laughing.

Frances said courteously, "Merry Christmas to you, too" and hung up before Betty's pricked-up ears could catch any more. "A girl from my office," she lied.

She looked at Mari, getting into her coat for the late dinner at her parents' home. Bill's attention was riveted to his cards; the wrinkles in his forehead deepened. Poor guy, she thought.

It was disturbing to see Bill this way; it annoyed her to think of him as needing pity. She had to admit that, viewed from some angles, the fault was at least partly hers. She stood beside him at the front door, shivering in the frosty air, when the Flanagans finally left.

But when they came back into the house, and he reached out to touch her, she moved away. "Please don't," she said coldly. "I'm tired."

He looked at her for a moment, without expression. Then he turned and went into the kitchen, dragging his feet. In a moment she heard the opening of the cupboard and the clink of glass against glass.

19

DON'T YOU THINK YOU'VE HAD ENOUGH?"

"For Christ's sake, baby, what is this, a Sunday school picnic?"

"Bake never knows when she's had enough," Jane said sharply. She moved her chair close to Bake's so that their shoulders were touching.

"Well, I can tell the difference." Frances stopped abruptly, realizing that it did no good to argue when Bake was like this; realizing too, that several people at nearby tables were looking curiously at them. She lowered her voice. "I'm sorry. Let's skip it."

"Like hell we'll skip it," Bake said. She looked narrowly at Frances, frowning, swaying a little with the intensity of her effort to focus. "It's none of your goddamn business how much I drink. And further—furthermore," she added, picking up her glass and looking around for the waitress, "Why don't you go home if you don't like it here? Nobody'd care."

Kay said, "Oh, for heaven's sake."

Jane was smiling a little. Bake said, "You can wipe that smile off your face, too. Another two-timer, that's what you are. Anything I can't stand, it's a two-timer. Me one day and Kay the next, that's the way you work it. You too," she said, pointing a trembling finger at Frances. "This gal's still sleeping with her husband, how do you like that? A straight girl. I don't know why they let her in a place like this."

Kay looked around uneasily. "We better go before Mickey throws us out, don't you think so?"

"God, yes," Frances said, "if we can get her away."

Kay raised her voice. "Look Bake, we're all going up to my place, okay? I'm going to the john first."

Frances followed her to the washroom. "I've never seen her this bad before," she said nervously. "Usually she gets loaded then passes out."

"Oh, this is typical. She's working up to a tantrum. I've seen it happen before—not for a long time though, not since you came on the scene." Kay took a small comb from her jacket pocket and carefully arranged her short hair. "Last time I was the one she was mad at."

"You were?"

"Sure. I asked her to stay away from Jane. It was the wrong thing to do, it only made her anxious to have Jane back." She looked into the mirror, running a finger along arched eyebrows. "You do know they're seeing each other again?"

"What did she say?"

"Oh, you know, the usual stuff. It's her life, nobody has any right to tell her what to do, and so on."

"Do you think it's serious between Jane and her?"

"I keep trying to tell myself it isn't. I don't know what I'd do."

"Jane means a lot to you, doesn't she?"

"I love her," Kay said simply. "Look, you and Bake have been together quite a while."

"A little over two years."

"I never knew Bake to stick to anybody that long. If that's any comfort."

"She used to go with Jane before. I know that." Frances tried to steady her voice.

"Sure. Jane was getting over Bake when I first met her. She was a mess—being dropped by Bake is quite an experience, in case you've never given it any thought."

"I know," Frances said in a muffled voice.

Kay's face was sad and a little stern. "We've been together four years, almost four and a half. Jane needs somebody to look after her. She's as helpless as a baby. She had analysis for more than a year after Bake threw her over. I hope to God the poor kid never has to go through anything like that again."

"I wonder—"

"Oh, there's nothing to wonder about," Kay said, dryly. "They'll try again. I think I've always known it."

"It seems so different when it's somebody else."

"I suppose all lesbians think they're different. I'm not cheap, I'm not promiscuous, it's different with us, we're not like the people you see in those cruddy places. Did you ever stop to think that's why we like to come to Karla's? Not be with our own kind, the way we keep telling ourselves, but to find somebody we can look down on. You come to a crummy joint like this and you think, well, anyhow we're different."

"We are different."

"Sure. We're discreet, we wear skirts."

"Sometimes I think Bake hates me."

"She probably does. Everybody has times of hating everybody else. I wouldn't worry about that right now," Kay said anxiously. "What I'm worrying about right now is how to get her out of here before something gives. It's not so long since umpteen people spent the night in the pokey because of her lousy temper."

"We can't just pick her up and carry her out, that's for sure."

"Funny thing is, when she's sober she's scared to death of the law. She was picked up and held for days once, and she still flips every time she thinks about it."

"I know. I found out the hard way."

"Sure."

"Maybe Jane could talk her into leaving?"

"Over my dead body. Jane'll go right along home with her if that happens."

"Do you think I'm happy about it?"

Kay smiled sourly. "Okay. I suppose nobody has any strings on Jane, either."

"The funny thing is, usually Bake hates to stay in one place. You just get settled down and she's ready to move on."

"Bake's running away from something," Kay said. "I don't know what. Maybe that's why we're what we are." She laid a warm hand on Frances. "Maybe that's why so many of us drink too much," she was sad. "That's a kind of running away too."

"That's true where I'm concerned. When I can't make up my mind about something, that's when I find myself getting fuzzy around the edges."

"Look," Kay said slowly, "it's none of my business, but if I had a husband and he was halfway decent to me—I used to be married, maybe you know, he was a worthless bum—but if I had a husband I could get along with, I think I'd stick with him. Maybe it isn't all moonlight and roses. Okay, so it's very romantic watching your girl get soused and make a public fool of herself. Not to mention the nights when you wake up and wonder how long you've got before she gets interested in someone else."

"I don't know," Frances said on a long sigh. "I don't know any answers. I'm afraid to look ahead."

Kay put a hand on her arm. "You're a nice kid. Let me know if I can do anything."

Frances gave her a watery smile. "What can anybody do?"

They went back into the crowded smoky room, arm in arm. Whatever ailed Bake, Frances decided as they got into their jackets and counted out the money for the drinks they'd had, it was building up to something major. Since Christmas, when she had refused to stay at the apartment, they had seen each other seven or eight times—roughly twice a week. Roughly was the right word too, she thought, remembering the bickering and recriminations, the way every contact ended with a quarrel in spite of her good resolutions not to fight with Bake.

True, Bake was drinking too much. She seemed to be spending more time at home than usual—January and February were slow months, she said, not meeting Frances's eyes—and she was drinking alone. Certainly she no longer stopped at one ritual martini, or two, when they lunched together.

But this was more than the temporary irritability that too much liquor aroused in her. That was a minor thing, annoying while it lasted but nothing to worry about. Since she was a busy and healthy girl, given to long walks and full of vitality, the physical damage was probably slight. Frances had learned to overlook her occasional lapses, since the others seemed to take them for granted. This was more serious.

"It's a kind of sickness," she said to Kay as they led their little party outside.

"Sure. Except she probably wouldn't see the only kind of doctor who could help her."

"But what is it?"

Kay shrugged. "How do I know? Maybe she feels guilty about something. Maybe she isn't getting what she wanted out of love. Maybe her mother hated her, for Christ's sake. All I know is, if you were smart you'd get out while the getting is good."

"Would you, if Jane got like this?"

Kay smiled tiredly. "Don't be silly."

The rest of the night was a weariness of alcohol, smoky air, and strident voices. Frances sat slumped at a small table in a strange room, thinking how off it was that bars mushroomed into existence and died again. She played with her glass and watched Bake and Jane drink. The hands of her watch crawled along with incredible slowness.

Kay said under her breath, "Nothing as dull as having a good time, is there?"

It was five o'clock when Bake finally fell asleep, with her head on the smeary table top. Kay winked at Frances. "Come on, let's get her out of here while she can still navigate. Janie, pay the man."

"What with, box tops?"

"You've got most of your paycheck left. I've been picking up the tab for you all night."

They waited while Jane fumbled out the money.

"Okay. Alley-oop!"

"She'll be madder than hell if she wakes up."

"She won't wake up," Jane said. She staggered a little herself as they reached the outside door and the cold air hit her in the face.

Bake's legs were rubbery, but she was able to walk after a fashion, with the other two steering and supporting her. They bundled her into the car, still almost asleep and muttering resentfully, and she vomited all over the backseat. Frances choked, watching her.

Kay rolled down the window. "I'm sorry, kid. Try to ignore it. She'll be all right as soon as we get her home and in bed."

Jane blinked owlishly. "I'll take care of her. I've taken care of her before. I know what to do."

Kay said steadily. "You've had about all you can handle, yourself."

"That's all right. I'll take care of her."

Kay glanced at Frances, warily, as though afraid to intrude on her private emotions. Frances sighed. "It's all right," she said in a small voice. "I'm tired of fighting all the time. Let her do it."

20 SOMETHING WAS THE MATTER WITH BOB. Frances observed his silence around the house, his diminished appetite—when an adolescent won't eat, the mothers in the office said, watch out!—and the small preoccupied pucker between his eyes, so like Bill's worried frown back in the days when Bill's mind was filled with human beings and their problems instead of sales quotas. Her first reaction was sharp annoyance—can't I ever have a moment's peace? The dormant maternal anxiety took over and she began to worry about his health.

He had been a sturdy youngster, recovering from the ordinary ailments of childhood easily. His cuts and bruises healed quickly, and he had never been inside a hospital except to have his tonsils out. She was both amused and chagrined at the fears that waited, grinning and gibbering, in the back of her mind. Polio, muscular dystrophy, epilepsy. She knew all this came from reading too many magazine articles, but it was all she could do not to take his temperature, just the same. And when she woke at night, sweating because she had just remembered a neighbor's child who died of leukemia, she had to fight off an inane impulse to tiptoe into his room and see if he was all right.

That he had no noticeable symptoms was some comfort. But not much.

Then it occurred to her that his trouble might not be physical. He's worried about something, she thought. That was worse, in a way; because what could he be worried about, and what could she do about it?

He had been a cheerful little boy who made friends easily. He had never come to her for sympathy, or, later, advice. Now and then, when he was small, she wondered if a girl might not be more companionable. Still, she was proud of him. He had adjusted to school, from kindergarten on. In clothes, behavior, and opinions he was practically a carbon copy of the other boys in his age group, and while grown-ups might be scornful of such conformity (even while they bought the things the advertising agencies wanted them to buy), it was evidently necessary to the young. Basketball, television, Saturday movies, ham radio, girls. He had a paper route at fourteen and delivered groceries at sixteen, like his pals. His mother had taken for granted that he was happy. She had enough to do, without fretting over imaginary problems, she reminded herself when some doubt of her motherly role nagged at her. Anyway, you can't do a thing for kids that age except see that they have clean clothes and enough to eat. They live in a world of their own.

Well-adjusted, that's what they call a boy who goes around with a nice bunch and does all right (two Bs and two Cs) in school. It was what she had wanted all through her hungry shabby adolescence—to belong. Now she wondered if it was enough.

Something's the matter with him, she thought, whisking through her Saturday housework. He's worried about something. Well, whatever it is, it's not my fault. He's had everything the other kids have. Bill's going to send him east to college—not Harvard, that's too expensive, maybe Dartmouth. She ran her dustmop around the edges of the living room rug, reflecting as she always did at this point in the weekly cleaning that when Bob's college fund no longer had to be considered, they would think about wall-to-wall carpeting.

He would leave in September, this was May. Four months. Then, as Bake was always pointing out, she could do anything she wanted to. She could, "live her own life."

But I'm not sure what my own life is, she thought, emptying

ashtrays and stacking them to carry to the kitchen. It certainly isn't keeping house. That's enough for some women, I guess, but it isn't what I want. When she married Bill, a well-kept house had been a symbol of everything she had missed as a child: security, standing in the community. But now the edge had worn off her need for security, and the people she had been seeing, the people whose approval meant something to her— Bake's crowd—had a different set of status symbols.

So fulfillment wasn't keeping house. And it wasn't adding up insurance premiums and writing form letters to remind people that their payments were past due. Most office jobs are a kind of housework, with a paycheck every two weeks to make them tolerable.

Books? At sixteen she had built a world out of them, only to have it shattered by the touch of Freddie Fischer's lips on her cheek. At thirty-five, trying to rebuild a universe of paper and printer's ink, she had met Bake and become engrossed in Bake's kind of love. She would always automatically reach out for anything with printing on it. But that wasn't enough, either.

She thumped the davenport cushions into shape and made her way to the kitchen, dustmop in one hand and piled ash trays in the other.

You're supposed to live for your children, she reminded herself, standing by the sink and looking vaguely at the breakfast dishes. For what? So they can grow up and go away from home, and leave you with nothing to do. Big deal.

As though her thoughts had materialized him, Bob came around the house and up the back steps.

Her heart contracted. To hide her concern, she piled dishes in the sink and turned on the hot water.

"Mom?"

"Hi." She had to ask; he was supposed to be at school, helping to decorate the gym for something or other, "Anything wrong?"

"Nope. What would be wrong?" He stood uncertainly in the doorway, a tall good-looking boy with a worried expression. "Dad home?"

"On Saturday morning?"

"Good old Saturday sales meeting, hah."

"Lunch will be late. Want a sandwich?"

"No, thanks. Look, Mom, I want to talk to you about something."

The urgency in his voice caused her to turn. He's grown up, she thought with an apprehensive tremor. As she would have done with a stranger she wiped her hands and led the way to the living room. There she sat down on the davenport and folded her hands to hide her sudden trembling.

Bob sat in the big chair, in the formal position of one about to be interviewed. There was a brief, embarrassing silence. Frances waited, intensely curious and unable to think what could be the matter.

Bob lit a cigarette. "Mom—"

"Yes."

"I've been talking to Mari."

She tensed at the girl's name, feeling her face grow rigid with self-control.

"We want to get married."

"Well, she's a nice girl. When you're through college—"

"Right away, maybe in June. As soon as we graduate."

"June! But that's next month."

"That's right." He hurried on, not looking at her, determined to say what he had to say and get it over with. "Her dad thinks he can get me a job in Michigan, for the summer, I mean. His brother runs a canning factory there. Mari could work in the office."

The inevitable suspicion took shape in her mind. "Why all the hurry?"

"No reason, except gosh, we don't see any point in waiting." He looked at her squarely now. "We're not in trouble or anything like that. We just want to be married while we're still young."

"You can't take a wife to Dartmouth."

"To hell with Dartmouth. We're going to Urbana—you

know, State U. They have housing for married students. It'll be cheaper, too. Mari has our budget all planned out."

Frances said coldly, "You're too young."

"Lots of couples do it. I talked to Dad. He's for it."

"Then why ask me?"

"Because." He crossed and uncrossed his knees, shifting uneasily in the cushioned chair. "Look, this is a pretty embarrassing thing to have to say to your own mother. I asked Dad to speak to you about it, but he won't. Lord knows it's his business as well as mine, but the old boy's pretty sentimental—"

Frances said abruptly, "I don't know what you're talking about."

"Sure you do. I guess that's what ails this family, all this hush-hush. Just like nobody knew about your friends. Or like it was a plague or something. This isn't the Middle Ages, they write books about people like that, for Christ sake. Mari showed me one, by some psychologist."

"Have you been discussing my personal affairs with Mari?"

"It's her business too, as much as anybody's. She says she can't marry me if you go on with this."

"With what?"

"Mom, for God's sake!"

"I'm sorry if you don't approve of my friends," Frances said icily, "or if your fiancée doesn't."

Bob leaned forward. "Look, you known damn well what I mean. If you want to run around with a bunch of female queers, that's all right with me—as long as you keep it private. It's no worse than sleeping around with other men, I guess, and plenty of married women do that. But when it comes to my mother being out all night with a bunch of lushes, and getting into drunken brawls and being tossed into jail—well, that makes it different. I know all about it, don't worry. Everybody knows, I guess, the neighbors and the people in Dad's office and all. Dad's been in hell."

"I'm sorry."

"Look, I wouldn't bring it up if it just involved me. It isn't so easy for a guy to talk to his mother about something like this." His voice was heavy with resentment. "Mari's scared her folks will find out."

Frances was unable to speak.

"Be reasonable," Bob said urgently. "In your day people married on impulse, that's why they had so many problems later. We know marriage isn't between two people, it involves others too. Man is a social being." Frances recognized this as a quote from the heavy green textbook used in the high-school course on Marriage and Family Relationships. "As long as you're going around with a lot of queers, Mari's folks will figure I'm a bad marriage risk. See?"

"You're too young. You're both too young."

"We want to make our adjustments early. Besides, we'd like at least four kids. This being an only child is for the birds."

Something was the matter with her mouth. Her lips were stiff and numb; it was difficult to form words. "What do you want me to do?"

"Settle down and act decent. Look," Bob said, "you don't belong with these people. You've got a good husband, you've brought up a kid. Maybe this is some kind of neurosis you've got. Okay, go and see a psychiatrist if you think it would do any good. Only for God's sake don't spoil my whole life!"

I suppose it does look like that from the outside, Frances thought. The tenderness and companionship—all overlooked. She said, "What about my life?"

Bob said brutally, "You've had your life."

She tried to smile. Feels like novocaine, she thought, just before it starts to wear off. "You won't think so, twenty years from now."

"Mother, you know what I mean." He looked at her pleadingly, without embarrassment. "Look, if you'll do this one thing I swear I'll never ask you for anything else."

So it was true. All the mushy movies and corny poetry, the stories in the women's magazines—they were right after all. You laid down your life for your children. When it came to a showdown, your common sense disappeared and some idiotic instinct took over and made you do things you knew were senseless. For the first time she understood all the smug mothers, the martyred mothers who "worked their fingers to the bone for their children," and were uninterested in life except as it concerned their offspring. With Bob's eyes (so like Bill's eyes as they had been during courtship) fixed on her, she had no defense against his need. Neither her envy of his girl nor her knowledge that he would fall in love with someone else in a few months if Mari rejected him was any protection against his naked need.

He said, muffled, "It's awful to be ashamed of your parents."

A thin child in faded gingham came to stand beside him, fixing her with big solemn eyes. Little Frankie Kirby, ashamed to go to school because her father was drunk again. She blinked hard to dispel the ghost.

"All right," she said flatly, "if it means that much to you."

"You won't see those—people anymore?"

"No."

"Or hang around the kind of places—"

"No."

"Gosh, Mom, you're swell. Mari'll be as grateful as anything."

Like hell she will, Frances thought. The young are never grateful, they take everything for granted. "It's all right."

"Those things generally don't last long anyway."

"Is that in the book, too?"

"Huh?"

"Never mind."

She sat there, unmoving, after he slammed happily out of the house. On his way to Mari's, she supposed, to make plans for the wedding. Her face felt wooden. She thought that she might break into small pieces if she tried to move.

Two years, she thought, automatically reaching back. Almost two and a half—this is May, that was November. (A small scarlet leaf against infinite blue, falling slowly.) He's right, that isn't very long. And I suppose we've already had the best of it. Hasn't been so good, lately.

She tried to recall the quarrels of the past few weeks, the sodden hours wasted in bars, the irritability she and Bake had developed toward each other. It was all unreal. It made no difference in the way she felt. She was in the apartment for the first time, sitting in front of the fireplace.

I love you. I think I've loved you for quite a while.

And later—much later, after the terror and the compulsion and the first scared, reluctant surrender and the incredible fulfillment—she had woke up, not knowing for just a moment where she was and what had happened. Then there was the sinking down into perfect happiness, with Bake's arm across her body and the darkness like a soft, warm blanket tucked in around the two of them.

She shook her head. I'll have to tell Bill, she thought. He'll be pleased. He has me right where he wants me, everything his own way.

But she made no move to stand up, because she knew that thought and feeling would come back when she moved, and that the pain would be bad.

21 SHE NEVER KNEW WHEN BOB TOLD BILL about that conversation. Perhaps he called the office from a pay phone, or perhaps—anger boiled up in her—from Mari's house, with her parents listening interestedly. He telephoned home to say that he and Mari were going out; he wouldn't be in until late. Ashamed to face her, maybe.

Bill brought the subject up at dinner that evening, looking at her thoughtfully across the kitchen table. "Bob say anything to you about wanting to get married this summer?"

She pushed the food around her plate. "Yes."

"It's a good idea, don't you think?"

"I guess so."

"Mari's a nice kid."

"Sure she is."

Never fight a daughter-in-law, never say a word that can

get back to her. She has all the weapons. She had heard them talking in the washrooms, the middle-aged women with grown children.

"Her folks are okay too. Her father's a circuit court judge. Nice people."

"I know."

Bill laid down the piece of bread he was buttering. His face was an odd mixture of expressions: exasperated and pleading. "I'm not so happy about this idea of changing schools."

"It's all right."

"Well, we're not getting any younger." He cut his chop. "Kid old enough to be married, and everything."

She couldn't help it, she was going to be sick. She pushed back her chair, its legs scraping along the linoleum. Bill jumped up. "Don't you feel good?"

"I'm all right."

He put his arms around her shoulders. The friendly touch dissolved all her antagonism. She wanted to cry. She turned her face away.

Bill said slowly, searching for words, "Looks like we haven't been getting along so well lately. Maybe that's my fault. Let's both try and do better, shall we?"

She moved away from him, out of the circle of his arms. "I'm going to bed."

"You want me to come up with you?"

She shook her head.

He stood looking after her, puzzled and a little sad. She shut the kitchen door behind her and went upstairs without looking back.

But in the bedroom—their bedroom—she felt restless and unable to sleep. She sat on the side of the bed, turning over a jumble of thoughts and feelings which refused to take on form. Bob, with that adult male look on his face. Bill, puzzled and hurt. Bake in a dozen familiar poses—incoherent with drink, curled up in sleep, swinging down Michigan Avenue with an armful of books, the wind from the lake ruffling her hair and blowing back her open coat.

I ought to feel terrible about all this, she thought. But she felt remote, as though it were happening to someone else.

She sat on the bed with her head bowed, unable to bring any order out of the chaos in her mind, until she heard Bill's step on the stairs. Then she threw off her clothes in a hurry and tumbled in between the sheets, shutting her eyes just as the bedroom door opened. He stood looking down at her. I'll scream if he touches me, she thought wildly. But he turned away from the bed without speaking, and went into the bathroom.

She lay awake for a long time after he came to bed, aware of all the night noises—cars going by, the clock ticking on the bedside stand, a breeze rattling the leafy branches of the tree just outside the window. She was aware, too, of Bill lying rigidly awake beside her. If she moved, he would speak to her. She wasn't ready to talk, not yet. She supposed they would have to discuss the situation—why in God's name can't anybody ever do anything without a lot of words?—but please, not tonight.

She controlled her breathing, and after a long time he went to sleep.

She woke late, to an empty bed and the indefinable feeling of Sunday morning. Bob had eaten and gone—he was taking Mari to church. His room was empty, the sheets and blankets in a tangle on the floor. She put on a housecoat and went downstairs. Bill was at the dinette table, still dressed in pajamas, drinking coffee. He filled a cup for her. She sat down, feeling a sharp nostalgia for the old days when Sunday morning had been their best time together.

"You mad at me?"

"No."

Her tone wasn't encouraging, but he tried again. "Look, I guess I haven't been a very good husband. If I'm to blame for all this, I'm sorry."

"It's all right."

"Anyway, it looks like a good time to make a new start. The boy's going to leave home. Going to get married. It's funny how much more important that seems than going to college, isn't it?" He shook his head wonderingly. "I guess that leaves us sort of depending on each other from here on in."

"Or free."

He stared at her. The slow color rose in his face. "Do you mean you want a divorce?"

If he had asked six months earlier, the question would have been a rainbow-colored miracle. Now she hesitated. The question of her leaving Bill and going to live with Bake had been dropped, tacitly, somewhere along the way. Bake brought it up sometimes when she had had too much to drink, because it was a very good solid grievance—she like to point out that she had been willing to pay the lawyer, even. Frances felt that Bake would be surprised and not too happy if she announced at this point that she was moving in. There was Jane, for one thing. Twice lately, when she had telephoned Bake's apartment, Jane had answered.

She shook her head. "I thought maybe you did," she said dully.

"Aw, Frankie, you know better. I'm willing to forget and forgive if you are." He hesitated, then decided not to be more explicit. "Maybe it's better this way than if you were mixed up with some other guy. I don't know."

"Don't talk nonsense."

"Well. Anyhow, I want you to know I'm sorry for what happened the other day."

She said again, "That's all right."

"Looks like it's time to make a new beginning, huh?"

She got up silently and refilled her cup.

"Forgive and forget, maybe."

"ALL RIGHT!"

Bill said mildly, "You don't have to holler at me. Anyhow, the Congdons are coming over this afternoon. To talk about the wedding."

Oh God, Frances thought. The bride's parents, coming over to size up the groom's family. Do you suppose she'll expect me to have jeans and a D.A. haircut like the gals at Karla's? She said crisply, "Thanks for letting me know. I have to sew a button on my blue crepe."

"Wear your pearls," Bill said, willing to put off the big reconciliation scene in favor of the immediate situation. "Make a good impression."

"I'll try. Get the good teapot down off the top shelf, will you?"

"Oh no, not tea."

Frances laughed.

But when she had found the blue dress, and thread to match, and even, miraculously, the button that had burst off several weeks earlier, she sat with everything on her lap and did nothing.

Nobody seems to know how it was, she thought rebelliously. They act like it was something shameful, or sordid, or evil. The fights and disappointments—well, but you get those with the other kind of love, too, and God knows you get them in marriage.

It was good, she told herself. Not all good, but mostly.

She didn't notice that she began to think in the past tense.

She sat with the dress across her knees, forgotten, staring at the wall of her living room.

22 FERNS AND SWEETHEART ROSES. LOHENGRIN. Chicken salad. Heirloom veil—Mrs. Congdon's grandmother's veil, no less, proving that the bride had ancestors. Double ring ceremony. Six bridesmaids in shades of yellow, ballet length. Mother of the bride in pale rose. Mrs. Congdon suggested, "Have you thought about beige lace for yourself, Frances? You'd be lovely in beige lace."

She had passed the inspection, with the help of the blue crepe and the best teapot. Had shown the guests out, smiling and gracious, and come back weak with relief—to find Bill pouring a long drink which he probably needed, but she was in no frame of mind to be reasonable. The quarrel that flared up was like a brush fire, crackling hot, soon over, leaving char and desolation in its passage.

He had been drinking too much ever since, not enough to keep him from going to the office, but evening after evening growing more flushed and silent, morning after morning getting up heavy-eyed and headachey. He spoke to her seldom, and then only on matters of necessity. And he had come home after a round of the night spots with a couple of customers, not only bloodshot and unsteady but looking guilty, the classic picture of the unfaithful husband. All that's lacking is lipstick on his shirt, she thought coldly.

Still, there was the wedding to get through. Nothing could be resolved before the wedding. They didn't discuss it, but there was a tacit understanding that everything else, including death if possible, would be postponed until the ceremony was over. In the meantime, it was necessary to keep the surface smooth and, above all, to keep the Congdons from finding out that all was not sweetness and light with Mari's future in-laws.

I don't want Bob to know either, Frances thought, panicking. Something like a prayer formed in her, finding expression not in words in a wordless resolution. Please, for Bob.

So here she was with Bill's check in her pocketbook and a feeling that she couldn't quite identify, a feeling that everything was coming to an end and nothing, apparently, would ever take its place.

"Too fancy," she said to the clerk. "Don't you have anything without all those ruffles?"

"I'll see." The woman sighed, walking away as though her feet hurt.

Frances stood, bored, knowing perfectly well that she would take the next dress she looked at, simply because it was ten minutes before closing time and the wedding was tomorrow. It would have been a good idea, she thought, for the kids to elope. Maybe she would bribe Bob—but a mental image of Louise Congdon shattered this notion. She sighed, shifting from one aching foot to the other.

"Frankie!"

She whirled around, almost knocking over the rack of "better dresses." "Kay, how are you?"

"Fine, fine. But what is the world are you doing up here with all the plush horses? Going into the movies, or something?"

Frances looked distastefully at the dress she had just refused to try on. "My son's being married tomorrow, and I haven't bought a dress yet. Her mother thinks beige lace—"

"My God, how suburban." Kay shook her head. "Come on, get it over with and we'll go somewhere for a drink. I haven't seen you for a long time."

"Come on back to the fitting room and give me a candid opinion. I've reached the point where I'm thinking of going in jeans."

In the green-curtained cubbyhole, Kay wedged her parcels onto the small shelf and lit a cigarette in defiance of the "No Smoking" sign above the mirror. "You look beat. Everything all right with you? Have you seen Bake lately?"

"Not for about three weeks."

They were silent while the saleswoman came in. Frances pulled the dress over her head. Then Kay answered the question she had been afraid to ask. "Jane and I have broken up, you know. I've seen it coming for quite a while—not that that makes it any easier."

"Has she—"

"I don't think so. Not officially, bag and baggage." Kay stood back a step and considered her critically. "Hey, that's not bad. I mean, I suppose you want to look like the groom's mother."

"I'd rather look like Zsa Zsa Gabor, but I don't seem to have the build for it."

"Go ahead, take it."

"I have to more or less. I mean, I've already bought all the stuff to go with it." She got out of the dress, allowing the waiting saleswoman to undo the tiny hooks at the side. "Thank God it won't have to be altered. Can you deliver it the first thing in the morning, without fail?"

"You can go in your bathrobe if they don't," Kay suggested. "Come on, I'll buy you a drink. I just cashed my salary check."

They came out of the store into late-afternoon June sunshine, sweet and hot. Kay carried her suit jacket over her arm; her forehead was beaded with perspiration.

"Hot, isn't it? Let's find a place that's air conditioned."

In the bar they relaxed, soothed by darkness and coolness, and looked at each other without any reservations. Frances said, "I'm sorry about you and Jane."

"These things happen." Kay's eyes were swollen and dark-ringed, she had lost five pounds, but she was under control. She smiled. "It's only—she was the first, you know. I didn't know, before. I was married, and then all of a sudden—"

"The same with me."

"I think she'll go back to Bake, eventually. I think this is what's been working out. Bake's been in some kind of spin, on the town every night, picking people up in bars. Riffraff, I mean. I only hope she gets it out of her system before she gets in real trouble."

The martinis came, in glasses wonderfully cold to the touch. Frances sipped hers absently. Kay said, "What are you going to do now, make up with your husband?"

"I don't know."

"Anything's better than being alone." Kay's smile hurt.

"After thirty you want something steady. I thought—I sort of hoped that was what I had."

Frances laid an impulsive hand on hers. "You're a swell girl."

"I like you, too. Want another drink?"

Frances didn't know whether it was the glow induced by two martinis, or the softening influence of sympathy, or the memories conjured up by seeing Kay; but after they parted she stood on the corner for a long time, stirred by an unreasonable impulse to call Bake. Might as well be friendly, she argued. I could call up and say hello, anyhow. A little light-headed, she went into a drugstore and waited her turn for a pay telephone.

"Bake? It's me."

"Well, for heaven's sake, where are you?"

"Corner of Adams and Wabash, in a Walgreen's. I just bought a horrible dress to wear to my child's wedding."

Bake said a little thickly, "Fine. Why don't we get together and have a drink to celebrate. Sort of a bachelor dinner."

She's been drinking, Frances thought. But the need to see Bake was urgent. She said doubtfully, "I have to be home early."

"Oh, come on. We'll go to Karla's and have just one, then you can go home in style in a taxi. Got an early-morning appointment myself."

"Okay. Just one though."

She was reminded of other evenings that had started with one drink and ended in bleary incoherence. I don't have to stay, she promised herself. I can be home by nine or so, get a good night's sleep—take some phenobarbital or a tranquilizer if Bill has any left over from that sales conference—can't afford to look tired tomorrow. Louise Congdon's probably having a manicure, facial, and permanent right this minute.

A car stopped at the curb and Bake got out, looking around.

If she had been living it up, it didn't show. But then, it never did. Bake's skin was clear, her tweed suit tidy. She smiled, and Frances's eyes misted. If we could only start over, she thought. If we could go back a year and do it over.

She said, "Look at me bawling. I've had two martinis already."

"All by yourself?"

"No, I bumped into Kay in Scott's."

"She told you she and Jane have busted up, I suppose."

"I was sorry to hear it."

"Kay's all right," Bake said frowning, "but she never really understood Jane. Jane's a sensitive person. Very shy, really."

She didn't want to talk about it. "Look, I have to go home early. One quick one, that's all."

"Sure."

But in the familiar clatter of Karla's, with Mickey bringing the drinks to their table to welcome them back, time seemed to stand still. Their first martini was followed by a second and then a third. It felt good to sit still and look at Bake's face, which was beginning to blur around the edges.

"My feet are tired," Frances said sadly. "This damn wedding."

"Poor baby."

"Got to go home pretty soon."

"Plenty of time. Let's have one more for goodbye."

Finally they went, forgetting to pay Mickey and then, when she called them back, having trouble counting the change. Frances felt happy and loose jointed. At the curb Bake said, "Look, let's go to The Pub. M-might amuse you. All full of girls in fly-front jeans."

"Bill's gonna be mad."

Bake scowled. "Bill own you, or something?"

"Hah."

The Pub, on the ragged edge of the theatrical district, was like a half dozen other bars she had visited with Bake's friends—a little darker, noisier, and more flyspecked, the glasses pyramided behind the bar not so shiny, and the percentage of shabby trousered customers higher than at Karla's or the Gay Eighties. In Frances's relaxed condition, it didn't matter. Tomorrow there would be the wedding to contend with, and after that a long stretch of nothingness. At the moment all that mattered was Bake, perched beside her at the bar, and the wonderful cool glass in her hand.

Got a lot of things to tell her, she thought foggily. Later, maybe. She felt that complete understanding was just beyond her reach; any minute now she would know all about everything, all the mysteries and inner meanings of life. She leaned close to Bake, willing to sit still and wait for a more complete revelation.

Bake said softly, "Look what just came in."

She squinted, trying to focus. The newcomers were five or six sturdy, muscular girls in tight slacks and striped jerseys, with visored caps pushed back off their foreheads. They found scattered places at the bar and ordered beer.

"Baseball team," Bake whispered, "girls pro baseball. The one on the end is sort of nice."

Frances looked, seeing nothing but a pallid blue. But the girl who had taken the stool next to her spoke up. "She's not so hot. Anyhow, she only goes for redheads."

This one was visible, at least. Bulky, not fat, but solid in her cotton pullover, with plump arms and a rather heavy face. No makeup. Under the pushed-back cap her hair curled springily. "Let me buy you both a drink. We just got paid."

Bake said, "We have to go."

"Oh, come on, be a pal."

"I'll have a beer," Frances said. She felt fine. Her view of the room blurred and softened, the outlines of people melting pleasantly into the background. When she turned her head, everything was fuzzy. She had to grip the edge of the bar with both hands and wait until her vision cleared. Bake gave her a warning look.

"Had enough," Frances began sleepily, agreeing, and then flinched as Bake swayed, put her head down beside her empty glass and went to sleep.

Frances's new friend said, "Jeez, she just passed out."

"Asleep is all. She does that."

"Won't she wake up?"

"Sure, after a while."

"Look, I got some good wine up at my place. Come along with me. We'll have just one."

Frances giggled. One with Kay, and one with Bake, and now one with this girl—the world was full of people with one drink. Funny arithmetic. She struggled to her feet, and the floor swung around.

"Money in my pocketbook," she said thickly.

"That's okay."

The bartender said, "A nice dish you got there."

"You can say that again." The girl slipped her hand through Frances's arm. "Come on, honey, it ain't very far. We can walk there."

It had gotten dark, somehow. Broad daylight when we came in here, she thought. The night was lit with street lamps that hurt her eyes. She clung to her new friend, sober enough to realize that the crossings were full of peril but unable to tell how far away the cars were or how fast they were coming. Her foot struck a curb, and she stumbled, then righted herself. An arm was around her, comforting and supporting her.

They turned in at a scabrous red brick house with torn dangling shades at the lighted windows. The girl pushed the door open. "Think you can make the stairs?"

"I'm fine. My friend Bake now, she had too mush—too much to drink." She gave up trying to explain.

It was important for this girl to know that Bake was the one who drank too much, but the stairs were steep and her foot kept slipping off the edge. She made the top with a triumphant feeling, and stood blinking as her new friend turned on an overhead light.

The room was a clutter of half-unpacked suitcases and duffle bags. A double bed filled most of it, and a folding cot had been set up against one wall. The girl kicked a shoe under the bed. "We just got in from Cleveland. We're going to be here three days—all but Maisie, she got a couple ribs busted this afternoon. I guess she'll be in the hospital a while." She began throwing things out of the largest suitcase. "Some of this junk is hers. Take your dress off and relax, honey. I sure hate to wear a dress."

"No time."

"Oh hell, it's a long time till morning."

Frances opened her mouth to explain that she couldn't stay until morning. There was some reason why she had to go home—she had forgotten what it was, but she knew it was a good reason. She had forgotten why she was here, too. She sat down groggily on the bed.

"Sleepy," she said.

"Why'n't you lay down?"

It seemed like a good idea. She stretched out warily, afraid of being dizzy again. But the girl was crooning to her now, little disjointed sounds and words of pleasure; her caresses were becoming more and more intimate and disturbing.

Frances stirred, dimly conscious of what was going to happen. "I can't."

"What did you come up here for, then?"

She didn't know. She tried to sit up, but the room went around in slow, sickening circles. Urgent hands were on her tender flesh and there was a smell of beer and tobacco and perspiration. She tried again to sit up.

The girl slapped her, hard. She cried out in pain and surprise, putting a hand to her stinging cheek.

"I'm sorry, honey. I'm sorry I had to do that. Now be nice."

Something was terribly wrong. This wasn't Bake, this wasn't the way it had always been. She lay back against the pillow, frightened and sick. Bake, she thought. Maybe if she screamed, Bake would come and help her. But she couldn't talk, there was a hand over her mouth, and everything was getting heavier and darker. Consciousness left her in little stabs and jerks, so that between moments of black oblivion she saw the dangling light bulb above her face, the clothes heaped on the floor. Then the roaring in her ears drowned everything else out.

23

COME ON, YOU, GET UP. YOU GOTTA GET OUT of here." Frances moved uneasily. Something was hurting her; she sensed it before she knew where she was or what was wrong. She turned her head, and pain ran in jagged streaks behind her eyes. She put out a blind exploring hand. Someone gripped her shoulder tightly. "Come on, damn it, wake up. You want cold water down your neck?"

She sat up wincing. Hangover, she decided with the slow, careful gravity that follows unaccustomed drunkenness. She had felt slightly ill two or three times before, when she had taken too much, but this all-over sickness was new. She turned over in bed, and was at once conscious of arches and stiffnesses here and there, physical in origin and owing nothing to alcohol. At the same time her eyes began to come into focus, and she identified the plain, heavy face of the girl who had bought her a glass of beer last night.

"Come on, come on, get goin'. I got practice in less'n an hour. You want some instant coffee?"

But where were her clothes? She wore only a slip, twisted and wrinkled, the lace torn across the top. She sat unsteadily on the edge of the bed, trying to collect her thoughts. "What time is it?"

"Half-past eight."

There was something special about this day, but she couldn't remember what. She stood up, pulling down the slip and noticing as she did so the bruises decorating her legs and abdomen. There was a tenderness around her left eye. She put up a careful hand and touched a painful, puffy mound of flesh.

"I'm sorry, kid. I oughta never touch anything but beer. Wine makes me ornery." The girl stirred coffee powder and hot tap water into two plastic cups, using a nail file as spoon. "You gave me kind of a rough time, though. What happened, lose your nerve?"

Frances didn't answer.

"I mean, you musta done it before. I wouldn't be the one to bring a girl out."

The coffee was bitter and not very hot, but she drank it. It gave her enough energy to get out of bed and sort out her own clothes from the mess on the floor. Pants, bra, stockings on bare feet. Her dress was wrinkled. A slip of yellow paper fell out of a pocket; she picked it up. Sales slip, receipted.

Oh God, the beige lace dress. The wedding. The wedding was today, high noon. She looked around wildly for her purse, found it on the dresser, and handed the plastic cup back to her hostess.

"Look. I have to get home. My son's being married at twelve o'clock."

The look that spread over the heavy face was one of helpless amazement. She stood aside without a word, and Frances clattered down the dusty thin-carpeted stairs, not caring who heard or saw her.

The street was quiet. But of course, in this neighborhood people would sleep until noon, at least. She stood on the curb beside a fire plug, willing every approaching car to be a taxi. Two of the baseball girls went by, looking at her curiously, and entered the house she had just left. Finally a Checker slowed down, and she got in and gave her address.

"Lady, that's way down on the South Side."

"Oh, please. It's an emergency."

The driver looked at her doubtfully, taking in the wrinkled dress, the puffy eye, the aroma that hung around her. But the light was green, and he shifted gears.

It was not until they were speeding smoothly down the Outer Drive that she wondered if she had enough money for so long a drive. She opened her bag, quietly. Lipstick, keys, a crumpled tissue. Her billfold was gone.

She said aloud, "the bitch."

"Huh?"

"Nothing."

For a moment she thought of asking him to turn back. But the girl would be gone, and even if she was there, she wouldn't admit to the theft. Besides, Frances thought, she might have dropped it on the street or left it at The Pub. (She thought fleetingly of Bake—what happened when she woke up, and did she get home all right?) A glimpse of a clock on the dashboard drove all thought of returning out of her mind. It was twenty minutes after nine. In two hours and forty minutes Bob's wedding would begin, with the bridegroom's mother unaccountably absent.

She leaned forward. "Can't you drive faster?"

"Look, you want to end up in hospital?"

Might be a good idea, she thought miserably. Solve everything. She sat on the edge of the seat, urging the vehicle forward with all her muscles, hating the whole human race and herself in particular.

Bill must have been waiting behind the living room curtains. He came running out before the taxi reached a full stop. She saw with rising hysteria that he was dressed for church. Gold links glittered in his cuffs, his tie was neatly knotted, his white shirt gleamed. He looked solid and solvent. She fought back a wild desire to laugh, or cry, or both.

"Pay the man, will you? I got slugged and rolled, just like in the movies."

He snapped open his billfold. "For heaven's sake, where have you been? Do you know what time it is?"

"I know. I told you, I was slugged." She didn't expect him to believe this, and it was evident from his face that he did not. After all, she had gone downtown in broad daylight, to buy a dress. "My dress! Did it come?"

"It's on your bed. If you're not ready in time Bob and I will have to go without you. Might be a good idea to gargle."

She said defensively, "I had one drink."

"I bet."

"Where's Bob?"

"In the living room, waiting to call the cops. On his wedding day."

She supposed she deserved that. Every step she took jarred her stiff muscles, made her bruises hurt more. Her back ached, and her legs were wooden. No time to think about that now. Later, if she lived through the wedding. And there was the reception too.

She moved toward the house as swiftly as she could, considering her pains. She was quite sober now, nauseated, her head aching and feeling utterly desolate. If this is how it feels to be hung over, she thought, it's a wonder everybody doesn't go out and join Alcoholics Anonymous right now.

But of course, everybody doesn't get slapped down and raped. She stood still, as the full implications of her situation got through to her.

Bill yelled, "For God's sake get moving! And do something about that eye!"

He'll kick me out for good, she thought, forcing her shaking legs to carry her up the porch steps. I'm no good. I've disgraced him and Bob. A tramp. Well, I'll worry about that later. I've got this wedding to get through, the Congdons and their damn Gold Coast relations. The mental image of Louise Congdon poised and critical, got her past the living-room door and up the stairs. Don't think about Bob, you'll fall apart. Don't think about anything.

As she hurried into the bathroom, she noticed that is was twenty-eight minutes after ten.

At ten minutes to twelve the mother of the groom walked slowly up the aisle of Holy Trinity Episcopal Church on the arm of the second-best usher, a rather flushed young man from Harvard who had certainly had a drink or two before breakfast. If her knees cracked at each step, if the pressure of a male hand on her beige lace sleeve made her wince, she managed to hide it. High headed, smiling, a little too lavishly made up (she could imagine the critical judgment of the bride's aunts and female cousins on this point), with a small brown feather hat pulled down over one eye, she was certainly younger and slimmer than many mothers of marriageable sons. She thought grimly that Mrs. Congdon, watching hawk eyed from the front right-hand pew, could find nothing to object to.

Unless, of course, it was the lavish hand with which dear Bob's mother had applied her perfume.

She concentrated on keeping her mouth shut, partly because the Listerine had proved only a temporary remedy for last night's breath and partly because, even though her stomach was certainly empty by this time, she felt a little uneasy inside.

Bill sat down beside her. She glanced at him, but his profile was stony. Bags under the eyes, too. He was certainly going to tell her off as soon as they got home. Maybe throw her out right away, with no money and no place to go. She guessed she had it coming.

The little rented house began to seem safe and familiar, even without a dining room.

She took a deep breath, careful to keep her lips pressed tightly together, and put the immediate future out of her mind. Nothing else mattered, if she could only get Bob married and off on his honeymoon. She could drop dead going down the church steps, and she wouldn't say one complaining word.

24 SHE AND BILL HAD STOOD UP TOGETHER IN front of a small-town preacher, chosen at random because they liked the looks of his small white church and matching parsonage, and because neither of them belonged to a church. Bill Ollenfield, whose job with the state welfare board didn't pay quite enough to support a wife, and skinny little Frances Kirby. There was a hole in the sole of her right pump, and she was afraid it would show when they knelt for the benediction. The witnesses were the minister's wife, in a housedress, and a neighbor lady who happened to be calling on her. And the wedding breakfast was coffee and hamburgers in a drugstore.

But the magic was there. Scared and guilty as she had been for the last few weeks, ever since her half-unwilling initiation into love (the hotel room was a dollar and a half, more than Bill could afford, and the night clerk had leered), when she looked into Bill's solemn face she felt untouched and bridal. For the space of a few minutes the parsonage living room was illuminated by a clear, shining light that transfigured everything. And when Bill took her cold trembling hand in his big warm one, her qualms vanished and she felt happier than she ever had before.

Now, in the candlelit quietness of Holy Trinity, she knew for the second time the sensation of reliving her own past. Standing beside Bill as the first strains of organ music filled the vaulted sanctuary, aware of the lacy whiteness that was Mari advancing slowly down the center aisle, she was at the same time standing in that shabby living room. Head bowed, she could see every detail of the rug, tan with faded red lozenges. The minister's thin, kind face glimmered through a sudden mist of tears. In a few minutes she would walk down the village street with her hand still in Bill's, proudly and soundly married, and he would look at her happily, but regretfully too.

"Frankie, I'm sorry we couldn't do it up right, with music and everything. I know it means a lot to a girl, having a church wedding."

"Silly, we're married. That's all that matters."

She actually had her mouth open to speak, here in church. Only the subdued turning of people around her, to look at the bride, covered the sound that had escaped her. She looked around quickly, avoiding Bill's eye.

And here was Bill—no, Bob, grown to his father's stature, very white faced and serious, coming out of the vestry with his best man, Mari's law school cousin. Time and place righted themselves. She was no longer Frances Kirby, at the threshold of grown-up life; she was Mrs. William Ollenfield, standing beside her husband, watching her only son get married.

She remembered the predicament she was in, and bent her head a little, hoping that neither the yellowish light of the candles nor the slanting blue-and-crimson rays that filtered through the stained-glass windows would rest on her swollen and discolored eye. Pancake makeup couldn't be expected to do miracles, after all.

How lovely Mari was, her eyes soft, her mouth tremulous as she passed down the aisle and met Bob before the altar. How young and tender—and how vulnerable. Pity flooded Frances's heart, washing away the last traces of resentment.

The attendants stepped back, leaving them side by side in front of the rector—and God, Frances thought, remembering her childhood belief that the Almighty dwelt exclusively in churches.

"Dearly beloved, we are gathered together—"

Tears welled in her eyes. Hampered by white gloves, she fumbled in her purse for a clean handkerchief. She was conscious of Bill's look, which she ignored. I suppose he'd like me to wipe my nose on my sleeve, she thought crossly, dabbing with the fancy bit of linen and lace.

She ventured a glance at him. Why, he wasn't glaring at all. His eyes were soft with pity and—she looked again, incredulous—something that could only be affection. She knew what it was, because it mirrored the emotion that suddenly overflowed her own heart.

"In the presence of God and these witnesses—"

She was afraid to look at him. Then, looking, she found herself unable to turn away. His gaze held hers.

As though he had told her in so many words, she knew that last night was no longer an issue between them. Out all night, drunk, promiscuous, raped, beaten, and robbed—degraded and faithless as she might be, still unsteady on her feet and marred by violence—it didn't matter. He was big enough to bypass it.

There wouldn't be any angry recriminations, any repudiation. There might not even be any discussion. He wouldn't ask for any promises. The matter would be settled by the simple fact of his forgiveness.

He loved her.

Never again, she thought in deep gratitude. I'll never look at anybody else. Man or woman. Give up the silly job, if he wants me to. Stay home and keep house. Or go back to school and take my degree. If he'll only take me back.

"Pronounce you man and wife."

It was over. How short a time it takes to get married, she thought, and how long it is before you find out what it really means.

She wiped her eyes, unashamed, as Mari put back her veil and lifted her face for Bob's kiss. Nobody noticed. Other women were crying, too, and some of the men wore that tight-jawed red-eared look that indicates suppressed emotion.

Louise Congdon's eyes were still pink when they met in the reception room. "A beautiful wedding," she said mistily. "We already love Bob like a son."

"We adore Mari, too." Frances gave her a wide smile. "If I only hadn't been stupid enough to bump into the bathroom door at the crack of dawn. I look like a prizefighter."

Because nothing mattered now, not even the faint, sickish, recurrent flavor of last night's liquor. What if she was bruised and battered? What if people looked and wondered? Bob was married, and Bill had forgiven her.

She was safe.

"Not at all, my dear, you look charming. I may be old-fashioned but I always think there's nothing like a piece of raw steak for a black eye. I remember when Mari was a youngster, it may seem unbelievable now but she was a terrible tomboy—"

Frances listened politely, smiled, turned to shake hands with Mari's spinster great-aunt from Milwaukee.

She kissed Mari and shook hands with Bob, whose greenish pallor had given way to a triumphant flush, and took her place in the receiving line without even bothering to pull the little brown feather hat down over her discolored eye.

People, and more people. Her legs ached, her arms were tired, there was a line of fire across her lower back whenever she bent. She thought, with no particular regret, that she had taken a real beating. The smile on her face felt wooden and silly. Bill looked pleased and tender, though. She guessed she was doing all right.

Faces of strangers, all with the same amiable and rather silly expression, put on for the occasion together with the dress-up clothes and white gloves. Frances shook hands, producing the right comments in rotation. I'm good, she thought smugly. I might have been doing this for years.

Suddenly, she felt the floor shake under her feet. For there was Kay, who certainly had not been invited, looking pretty and conventional, in hat and heels, with a mink stole (Jane's) slung over her shoulders. She made her way down the line, shaking hands. Frances's heartbeat quickened. Here was everything she was leaving behind—rapture, heartbreak, the exciting potential of a new affair.

Kay reached her, raised her eyebrows at sight of the bruised eye, then winked and moved on.

She's a wonderful person, Frances thought forlornly, watching her retreating back. Warm. Understanding. We like the same books and the same people. I could tell her everything and she wouldn't be shocked or disapproving, the way some people are. I wish I knew her better.

Like a slap in the face came the realization that while she wanted Kay as a friend—nothing more, nothing else—Kay's thoughts of her, now visibly budding into plans, involved a great deal more than friendship.

She shot another look at Bill, standing beside her with his head bent, listening courteously to a shrill old harridan in purple chiffon. What she saw was reassuring. What if he was getting a double chin? What if his hairline was beginning to recede? He was Bill. Dear, familiar, safe, the stuff of day-by-day living.

After all, she admonished herself, life isn't made up of romance. (And Kay was right, there was nothing so very romantic in watching someone you love get drunk and make a fool of herself.) If you got one good, exciting, adventurous episode out of a lifetime, you were probably doing better than average.

She turned for a valedictory look at Kay, now half-hidden in a milling throng of friends and relatives.

Well, I'm not sorry. It was good, and I'll stick to that no matter what. (A pang hit her somewhere in the midriff. Bake, darling.)

"Tired?"

"Hm? Oh, not so very."

"Won't be long now. The lunch is set for one-thirty." He glanced at his watch. "Should be able to break away around half-past three, at the latest. I don't have to go to the office," he added grinning. "I'll stay home and keep you company."

Her eyes widened. Full realization of what this reconciliation would mean in terms of her relationship with Bill struck her for the first time. His tone, the look he gave her—there was no question about it. This wasn't going to be any platonic marriage.

Well, why not?

Beneath all the fatigue and stiffness, the aches, the nausea and bewilderment, a familiar need was beginning to clamor in her. After all, she thought, shaking hands absently with a stern-looking man, it's been a long time.

The corners of her mouth twitched into a smile.

It would feel good to get home, cold cream the gunk off her face, and take off her shoes, maybe crawl under her own covers for a nap. I need some rest, she thought, feeling very bright to have figured that out. Then I can make up my mind what to do next.

But she knew, glancing upward at Bill's profile, that her mind was made up.

The days and nights reaching ahead were, after all, full of glowing possibilities.

There was the matter of Kay. She would call—she knew the number, she had called before, when Bake was sick. As though Kay's face were within her range of vision, Frances could see her winged eyebrows pulled together in planning.

With only a minimal qualm, she renounced Kay's friendship and whatever possibilities it might hold of emotional involvement. I'll leave the receiver off the hook, she decided firmly.

Bill smiled down at her. "Want to go somewhere and sit down?"

She slipped her hand into his. "All I want," she said softly, "is to go home—with you."

THE END

AFTERWORD
The Stuff of Day-by-Day Living

ONE CAN ONLY IMAGINE THE REACTION OF A woman in the early 1960s, stopping at the drug store for a new paperback novel to entertain her after a hard day at work and finding that the central character is a depressed housewife, a victim of incest, a raging alcoholic, or a survivor of the sexual and emotional horrors of a World War II concentration camp. In *Stranger on Lesbos,* her pioneering 1960 novel, best-selling pulp novelist Valerie Taylor provided tantalizing glimpses of a secret, subterranean alternative to mainstream American life as well as the costs involved in choosing it.

Lesbian pulp novels have been described as having certain recognizable characteristics: published between 1950 and 1965 as mass-market paperbacks, they include some lesbian content and have cover art or copy that screams "sexy girls having sex together!"[1] This new and sensationally successful genre emerged in the early 1950s at the same time that a new lesbian identity also tentatively emerged. By mid-decade, groups like the San Francisco-based Daughters of Bilitis (DOB) helped to provide a sense of connection, and the beginnings of community, to women who desired other women; they also helped the

1. Valerie Taylor, *Stranger on Lesbos.* (orig. pub. by Gold Medal Books, 1960); Kate Brandt, "Valerie Taylor: Writing Since the 1950s and Still Going Strong," in *Happy Endings: Lesbian Writers Talk About their Lives and Work* (Tallahassee, FL: Naiad Press, 1993), as reprinted in Valerie Taylor, *Whisper Their Love* (Vancouver: Arsenal Pulp Press, 2006; orig. pub. by Fawcett.

writers of pro-lesbian pulps find their audience. Nineteen fifty-seven was the groundbreaking year of what publisher Barbara Grier defined as the "golden age of lesbian pulps."[2] Years later, Taylor remembered, "there was suddenly a plethora of them on sale in drugstores and bookstores . . . many written by men who had never knowingly spoken to a lesbian. Wish fulfillment stuff, pure erotic daydreaming. I wanted to make some money, of course, but I also thought that we should have some stories about real people."[3]

She succeeded beautifully, with one caveat: the "real people" in Taylor's lesbian novels, most of whom are richly drawn and incredibly complex females, also incorporate a wide range of human experiences, some of them stark and upsetting. While sharing the excitement and sensuality of lesbian relationships, Taylor also explored "the stuff of day-by-day living" which included the sad, scarred, and self-destructive aspects of her heroines' lives. She refused to sugarcoat the difficulties of going against the grain.[4]

Taylor's early lesbian-themed work sprang organically from her interest in three very different characters, each of whom felt trapped by her surroundings, her past, and her inability to fit into current social norms. *Stranger on Lesbos* introduced unhappy housewife Frances Ollenfeld to the joys and despairs of lesbian love and began a series of novels featuring strong, intelligent, and attractive young white women who struggle with their sexual desires for other women in a climate of misogyny, homophobia, substance abuse, and sexual violence. The second book in the series, *A World Without Men* (1963), introduces Erika Frohmann, still suffering from the aftereffects of repeated rapes and horrible depravations during her wartime internment. In *Return to Lesbos,* also originally published in 1963, Frances Ollenfeld and Erika Frohmann meet and fall in love; *Journey to*

---

2. Yvonne Keller, "'Was It Right to Love Her Brother's Wife So Passionately?' Lesbian Pulp Novels and U.S. Lesbian Identity, 1950–1965" (*American Quarterly*, Volume 57, No. 2, June 2005): 396. See also Irene Wolt, "An Interview with Valerie Taylor," *The Lesbian Review of Books*, Vol. 14, No. 3, Spring 1998.

3. Keller, 388.

4. Ibid. 392.

Fulfillment (1964) goes back in time to describe Erika's teen-aged years and her arrival in the Chicago area postwar. *Ripening* (1988), the sequel, brings Frances and Erika to Tucson, Arizona to live among a new generation of lesbian activists, family, and community— much like Taylor herself had done.

BORN VELMA NACELLA YOUNG IN AURORA, ILLINOIS, on September 7, 1913, Valerie Taylor died in Tucson, Arizona, at the age of eighty-four, on October 22, 1997. In a 1988 interview, she said that she created the name "Valerie Taylor" when she began selling stories in the early 1950s because her husband did not like her publishing under her married name, which was Velma Tate. She also used the name Nacella Young and as such published approximately two hundred poems, starting in 1946 and continuing through the 1950s and early 1960s. By the 1970s she was known as Valerie Taylor.[5]

She chose "Valerie" because it means "brave or courageous" and she says she picked Taylor "out of the air" because she wanted to keep the same last initial (T). However, she continued to use the name Velma Tate for legal purposes or, as she put it, "voting and Medicare," after her divorce in 1953 from Bill Tate, who suffered from alcoholism and heroin addiction. She also used it when she was involved with the Chicago chapter of DOB for a few years in the early 1960s and published poems and essays in *The Ladder,* DOB's monthly magazine, which was the only national publication by lesbians and for lesbians until the late 1960s. Taylor published in *The Ladder* from 1961 to 1965, and it was through the DOB/*Ladder* connection that she came to know Barbara Grier, the longtime literary editor of the magazine.[6]

After her divorce from Tate, she lived independently, struggling to make ends meet as she raised her three sons in the Chi-

5. Tee Corinne and Caroline Overman, "Valerie Taylor Interview," *Common Lives/Lesbian Lives* No. 25, Winter 1988: 23–34.
6. Tee Corinne, *Valerie Taylor: A Resource Book*, The Estate of Valerie Taylor, 1999; Valerie Taylor Papers, Rare and Manuscript Collections (RMC), Cornell University Library, Ithaca, NY.

cago area throughout the 1950s and 1960s. Taylor had begun writing for the "true confessions" market at night and working in a variety of offices and other workplaces during the day. From 1957 to 1964 she helped kick-start the quickly expanding paperback originals market, publishing seven lesbian-themed novels in as many years.[7]

In 1963, arguably her most prolific year, Taylor fell in love with attorney Pearl M. Hart, whom she described as "the great love of her life." Hart, a well-known Chicago civil rights lawyer, was a founder of the radical National Lawyers Guild. Together they helped start the gay rights group Mattachine Midwest in 1965 after the Chicago chapter of the DOB went dormant. Their years together were not easy ones. Taylor adored her lover despite Hart maintaining a long-term relationship with another woman, a local actress. Taylor also was active in local politics as well as the Chicago chapter of the Women's International League for Peace and Freedom, which she had joined as an open lesbian during the Vietnam War era. In 1974, as feminist and lesbian liberation movements expanded, Taylor worked with Chicago activist Marie Kuda and others to launch the annual Lesbian Writers Conference. The conferences met for the next five years and provided a much-needed lavender lifeline for lesbian writers. They also promoted the small presses then publishing novels centered on women-loving women—like Kuda's short-lived Womanpress as well as Grier's Naiad Press, which reprinted three of Taylor's lesbian paperback novels— and introduced the pulps, and some of their authors, to a new generation of women.

After Hart died of cancer in 1975, Taylor left Chicago for the small town of Margaretville, New York, not far from Albany. Fearing her increasingly closeted existence in small-town upstate New York, Taylor left Margaretville and moved to Tucson, Arizona in 1979; there she reconnected to both literary and lesbian communities. In addition to continuing her activist

7. Marcia Gallo, "Eight Kinds of Strength: A Tribute to Valerie Taylor, Lesbian Writer and Revolutionary," *New Politics* Vol. XII, No. 2 (Winter 2009): 136–139.

involvements as a "gay Grey Panther," becoming a Quaker, and falling in love again as she neared the age of seventy, Taylor continued to write poetry and novels, including *Love Images* in 1977, *Prism* in 1981, *Ripening* in 1988, and *Rice and Beans* in 1989. She was inducted into Chicago's Gay and Lesbian Hall of Fame in 1992. An interview done just two years before she died can be found in famed oral historian Studs Terkel's 1995 book *Coming of Age: The Story of Our Century by Those Who've Lived It.*[8]

Unique among both pulp novelists and women writers of her era, Valerie Taylor was able to creatively incorporate her radical politics with lesbian feminism and her marketable craft of storytelling. She used her talents to promote new ideas: "there are always books in my books," she would say, acknowledging her habit of referencing other lesbian writers as well as her own works within her stories. There are always bits and pieces of contemporary controversial issues in them, too, scattered like breadcrumbs in the forest for hungry fellow or sister travelers. As she said in 1993, "I like to write about the kind of people I like to know." In *Stranger on Lesbos,* we meet some of the people she knew. It is an early-1960s world full of complicated women, captured as she saw them then and including the sexual and social challenges of that era more than fifty years ago, yet still relevant today.

—Marcia M. Gallo
2012

8. Marie Kuda, correspondence with author, February 19, 2012; Chicago Gay and Lesbian Hall of Fame, *http://www.glhalloffame.org*; Studs Terkel. "Valerie Taylor, 79" in *Coming of Age: Growing Up in the Twentieth Century* (New York: The New Press, 1995: 307–314). See also John D'Emilio, "A Woman For All Generations," *Windy City Times* August 6, 2008; *http://www.OutHistory.org*

The Feminist Press is an independent nonprofit literary publisher that promotes freedom of expression and social justice. We publish exciting authors who share an activist spirit and a belief in choice and equality. Founded in 1970, we began by rescuing "lost" works by writers such as Zora Neale Hurston and Charlotte Perkins Gilman, and established our publishing program with books by American writers of diverse racial and class backgrounds. Since then we have also been bringing works from around the world to North American readers. We seek out innovative, often surprising books that tell a different story.

See our complete list of books at **feministpress.org**, and join the Friends of FP to receive all our books at a great discount.

THE FEMINIST PRESS
AT THE CITY UNIVERSITY OF NEW YORK
FEMINISTPRESS.ORG